Praise for Melanie Hooyenga's

FLICKER

"Hooyenga's FLICKER had me on the edge of my seat! A great who-done-it for YA fans, it had me guessing until the very end. Hooyenga had me (and my teenage daughter who loves this book) eyeing the shadows between trees a bit differently after reading FLICKER, it stays with you long after the last page."

—STACEY GRAHAM, author of The Girls' Ghost-Hunting Guide and The Zombie Tarot

"The story moves at a quick pace as you're drawn into Biz's world right from the first page, and an intriguing world at that. One that blends paranormal elements seamlessly into everyday life, before taking you into the depths of a mystery with an unexpected climax. Above all, Biz's thoughts and experiences shine through on each page, giving her character an authenticity that will connect you with the story and her life. Also, the author honors her readers by wrapping up loose ends before teasing with what's to come in the sequel 'Fracture.' Overall, 'Flicker' is a fantastic YA novel."

—BELLA BOWIE

"This certainly made me a lover of YA! I can't wait to see what Melanie has in store for us next!"

—JUNE KRAMIN, women's fiction author

"As a 39-year-old man with several teenaged children, I feel qualified to say that 'Flicker' is a book with the potential to produce a true genre-busting YA franchise."

—SCOTT BREW

By Melanie Hooyenga

FLICKER

FRACTURE

FRACTURE

Melanie Hooyenga

Left-Handed Mitten
Publications

FRACTURE

Published by Left-Handed Mitten Publications

ISBN 1500214418
eBook ISBN 978-1500214418

UPC

Book design by the Ink Slinger Designs
Cover design by Ink Slinger Designs
Ebook formatting by Ink Slinger Designs
Author photo by Jenn Marie Photography

Author website: www.melaniehoo.com
Email: melaniehooyenga@gmail.com
Facebook: facebook.com/MelanieHooyenga
Twitter: @melaniehoo

For my dad, who passed too soon,
but filled my life with love

Chapter 1

Before last month I never gave much thought to my school's no-hats-during-school-hours policy, but all that changed after Martinez shaved my head.

The final bell rings and I smooth my knit hat over my head, tugging it firmly to my ears. The pressure from my chest that builds every day, all day, eases out of me in one long exhale. I rise with the other students and follow them into the hallway, wishing for the bazillionth time that Stride Right—Mr. Walker, the principal—had cut me some slack.

No one stares as I weave through the hall to my locker, but my fingers find their way to the edge of my hat anyway. They lower as I see Cameron leaning against my locker, one foot propped against the scuffed metal.

"How long you gonna wear that?" He pushes off the locker and I tuck myself against his chest. "No one cares."

Before I can catch myself, my fingers slide beneath the hat to trace the scar that zig-zags across my skull. "I care." I wish I didn't, but I do. Curse of being seventeen.

Cameron presses a kiss to my forehead, just beneath the edge of my hat. His warm lips send tingles through my stomach.

"Well maybe if you did that through all my classes I wouldn't mind so much." As much as I hate to, I pull away and open my locker. I shove books in my bag as Cameron laughs.

"I'm sure Stride Right will be totally cool with that."

I sling my bag over my shoulder and we fall in step toward the exit.

Cameron grabs my hand, gives it a little squeeze. "You think today's finally the day?"

"I'll get Martinez to agree if I have to beat him over the head with a chair. Being ferried by my mom is getting really old." Cameron opens his mouth but I stop him. "I know you offered to drive, but this is her way of taking care of me. There isn't much else she can do."

"You think he'll agree?"

I shrug. "Probably not."

We follow a group of students out the front door of the school and walk slowly toward the end of the pick-up lane. Humiliation washes over me, warming my neck and creeping over my face. It's bad enough they shaved my fricking head. Martinez insisted that surgery was the only way to control the mass in my brain, but losing my driving privileges is beyond ridiculous.

As if sensing my thoughts, Cameron lowers his head and kisses me quickly on the lips. I slide my hands behind his neck, not ready to let him get away just yet, but the sharp blast of a car horn stops me.

Cameron smiles. "Busted."

I press one last kiss to his cheek then hurry to meet Mom. "I'll see you in a couple hours."

*****

"Biz, you know the risks." Dr. Martinez sits less than a foot away on a rolling stool, elbows on knees, chin resting thoughtfully on his fists. This does not look promising.

"But Mom can't be driving me everywhere. She's already missed enough work..." I trail off, hoping the desperation in my voice is enough to convince him.

Mom looks away, avoiding my gaze. I cast a glance at the empty chair next to her, but Dad isn't here to argue in my defense. A flutter of worry turns in my stomach. Mom would've said if something had happened. He's probably just tired. As usual.

Martinez holds up his hands in protest, but his ramrod straight posture is crumbling. He's giving in. "Okay. But only on a limited basis. No driving at night, just to and from school. You'll get another CT scan next month and if everything comes back clear you can have full driving privileges."

I straighten in my chair. "Really? You'll let me drive?"

"You had major surgery and you can't expect to go back to your normal routine overnight." He keeps talking, but I'm no longer listening. I can drive!

Mom's lips curve into a smile. Dark circles ring her eyes and the lines in her forehead are deeper than they were a month ago. I swallow my excitement and try to calm down. It's bad enough she has to worry about Dad; I hate that I'm adding to her stress.

"I know this is boring for you, but I need to go through the checklist." He grabs the clipboard from the corner of the counter and I rise from my chair. Place my feet together, knees slightly bent. Close my eyes. For a brief moment Cameron and his sister Katie—the reason I had surgery and am standing in this office—dance before me. My stomach clenches.

"Lift your left foot."

I do.

"Touch your right hand to your left ear."

I lift my right hand and—no! I didn't hesitate. That wasn't a hesitation. I crack an eye open. Martinez is staring at the clipboard, pen bouncing between his thumb and forefinger. My fingers brush my ear and he nods.

"Now the other foot."

We go through this for the next ten minutes. Him trying to trip me up, testing my brain. Me doing my damnedest to pay attention and not make a stupid mistake.

"Last one." The pen clicks—open, shut, open—then he clears his throat. "Point your left foot toward me, then toward the back wall, then toward me again." I steady my breathing, determined not to tip over, and follow his commands. "Now shake it all around."

What the—? I open my eyes.

A broad smile stretches across Martinez's face.

"The hokey pokey?" I face Mom. "Did you put him up to this?"

Her giggle is contagious and a snort erupts from me. "I hate you," I say to Martinez.

"Yeah, yeah. Join the club."

This is why I haven't killed Martinez for shaving my head. Yet.

Chapter 2

I knock on Cameron's front door as Mom rolls out of the driveway. This is our compromise. My eighteenth birthday is in three months, yet she refuses to leave until she knows I'm safely inside. A slow backward exit seems to appease her.

Cameron opens the door and I slip inside. The lingering aroma of tomato sauce and garlic makes my stomach growl, despite the fact that I just ate. Mom's a great cook, but with Dad in bed more and more and her carting me all over town, our meals have turned into a game of Name that Frozen Dinner.

"How'd it go?" he asks.

I give him a quick hug. "I get to drive!"

"Really? That's awesome. No more mom shuttles?"

"Nope." I follow him into the living room, still smiling. "The appointment wasn't bad, but Martinez thought'd it be fun to make me dance like a monkey." Cam laughs as I explain, but the sound dies as we stop next to the couch.

Katie sits hunched on the far end of the couch. A textbook lies open on her lap, but she's staring at a space behind the TV.

"Hey, Katie," I say softly. I've seen her almost every day for the past month—since they released me from the hospital—but I can't accept that this shell of a girl is the same bouncy, happy child that used to follow me and Cameron everywhere. Four years is a long time to be apart from your family—she basically grew up locked in a cabin in the woods—and while I know it's ridiculous to think that escaping her captor would flip a switch and she'd go back to the Katie we used to know, I wish there was a way to do more, to help make her transition to the normal world a little easier.

Her head jerks in my direction—a nervous reaction that greets any new person to the room—and her eyes linger a moment before drifting back to the wall. "Hey."

My mood falters. It's naive to hope otherwise, but I keep

forgetting that the Katie who used to adore me doesn't exist anymore.

Cameron touches my back. "Did you eat yet? Mom's making spaghetti."

I'm tempted to lie but I don't think I could fake my normal appetite. "I already ate. I can start my homework while you guys eat." I sink onto the couch, careful not to jostle Katie, and unzip my backpack.

"I'm not hungry either." Katie's voice is flat, monotone.

"Do you want to watch a movie?" Cameron asks.

I cringe at the desperation in his voice. He's trying so hard to accommodate this new Katie that he jumps at any small thread she gives him. If she was anyone else I might think she's trying to manipulate her brother, but I don't want to believe that of her.

Katie shrugs. "Can I pick?"

I reach for the remote but she grabs it before I touch it, and her quickness startles me. She's mastered the art of fading into the background of a room so well that I sometimes forget she's there. If you can ever actually forget that a girl who was missing for years and is suddenly returned is still in the room.

Cameron's parents didn't inject her with a homing device, but I have a feeling they would if it was an option.

Katie switches the channel and a ghostly face surrounded with strobing lights fills the screen.

"Ugh." The sound escapes my mouth before I can stop myself.

"What, you don't like this?" I swear a smirk slips across Katie's lips. She's less than a year away from officially being a teenager and she's already mastered the attitude.

Cam rubs the top of my head and says "The lights bug her eyes," at the same time that I tap the side of my skull and say "Headaches."

Katie smiles, but doesn't change the channel. "At least I'm not the only freak around here."

*****

As the hero standing gasps a final breath and the killer limps off into the sunset, a buzzing against my leg makes me jump for the hundredth time in the past hour. Cameron laughs as he reaches between us for his phone.

I blush, but not because of Cameron. He knows I hate

horror flicks. "I don't know how people watch scary movies."

He brushes my neck with his fingers while his other hand scrolls through a text. I don't want to pry so I look at Katie, who's watching us.

"It's a distraction from the real world." Her hands rest in her lap, unlike Cameron, whose thumb flies over the tiny keyboard. Her phone buzzed several times during the movie but she's yet to pick it up.

"I guess." I'm rarely at a loss for words, but talking to Katie has become more challenging the longer she's been home. Everyone keeps saying "we need to be patient while she readjusts" and I totally get that. The nightmare Katie lived through for the past four years is worse than anything we could watch in a movie, but tact isn't my best quality and several times I've had to bite back a snarky comment before it leapt from my mouth and smacked her on the back of her dyed-black head. Nothing I say could possibly make things worse, and tip-toeing around her has to drive her crazy, but for now I take extra care to watch what I say.

Cameron sets his phone on the couch and I can't help myself.

"Who was that?"

"Huh? Oh…" he glances at his phone. "One of the family members from…" he tilts his head ever-so-slightly in Katie's direction, trying to be subtle, but Katie sees it. Her fingers flex against her thighs, the only movement she makes. "It's not a big deal." He leans his head against the back of the couch and slowly exhales.

I wait for him to say something else but he remains quiet. This isn't the first time people from the Rescued Girls group—that's what the media started calling Katie and the other three girls who were found alive thanks to my whacked-out brain—have texted him, and I get why he doesn't want to get into it in front of Katie. She doesn't always react well when people fuss over her—flipping out would be putting it mildly—so he probably thinks he's making it easier on all of us by not elaborating, but—

"You're arguing with yourself again." Cameron nudges me in the side. Usually this is a sure-fire way to make me smile. Before we even started dating, back when we were just friends lusting for each other, Cameron could always tell when I was struggling with something.

22

But this time I don't smile.

He nudges me again. "Hey, you okay?"

I nod against his shoulder, not sure how to explain what's bothering me, but there's no ignoring the knot that's clenching my gut or the nervous sweat that beads above my lip. I drag the back of my hand over my mouth before he notices, hoping I'm wrong.

Hoping it isn't Sarah that keeps texting.

It makes sense that they became friends. After the girls came home, while I was recovering from surgery, the families formed an unofficial support group, meeting in each other's homes and learning to depend on one another. I've known about Sarah from the beginning. When Cameron visited me while I was in the hospital—smuggling in cheeseburgers and orange soda when I couldn't take another day of the food— he shared the stories from the group, and mentioned her several times.

He's allowed to have other friends.

So why do I feel so uneasy?

Chapter 3

"Biz, when are you going to quit with the hat? Your hair looks fine." Amelia, my best friend and the only person I can't say no to, pulls her long ponytail in front of her face to inspect it closer. "In fact, I was thinking of chopping mine off, too."

I slam my locker shut and wait for the giggle, but she just stares me straight in the eye. "You're not cutting your hair. It's bad enough one of us has to look like a cancer patient."

She punches me in the shoulder. "Stop. It's really cute. You just need to add some product..." her fingers brush through the hair that's just beginning to curl on top and I swat her away.

"Come on, we'll be late for class."

Despite all my hopes, having brain surgery and getting

kidnapped did not excuse me from Trig hell. Although technically no one knows that I was kidnapped—only my dad and Cameron know that minor detail. Two months ago was the last time I flickered—used sunlight to go back in time to yesterday—and I did it to try to stop a little girl from getting kidnapped. But I never stopped to think that I might get snatched, and I certainly didn't expect that the kidnapper who had eluded the police for years would turn out to be my favorite teacher, Mr. Turner. I managed to flicker out of his van before he got me to the house where he'd kept Katie and the other girls, then my dad called in a tip to the police that ended up saving the girls. It's an incredible story, but no one knows it happened. All the kids at school know is they poked around in my brain and gave me this fabulous haircut.

*****

After class I head back to my locker to grab my jacket and my gut sinks. No Cameron. He's always waiting for me after Trig, so why isn't he here now? I toe the random papers at the bottom of my locker, check that my car keys are in my jeans pocket, and glance over my shoulder down the hall. Kids swirl around me, all heading to their next class and hardly concerned with the weird bald chick who can't find her boyfriend, but I don't want to look desperate.

One minute. I'll wait one minute, then I'll leave without him.

Okay, I guess I'm leaving without him.

Shelly, the make-shift instructor of my photography class, is pretty cool if we're not there on time, but Cameron and I have been late a couple other times when we... well, let's just say sometimes a girl likes to be alone with her boyfriend. Considering that she's doing extra work just to help us, I don't want to piss her off.

I pull into a spot in the visitor lot at the Daily Chronicle, which means I'm not the last one here. Old Berta, Cameron's ugly orange car, is nowhere to be seen. Whatever, I'm sure he'll be here soon. I grab my camera bag and hurry through the front doors.

"Biz, hey!" Shelly Graham waves from her perch on a long table on one end of the room. Petite with a dark pixie cut that's longer in the front so it falls over her eyes, she's the type of girl—woman—who seems to have it all figured out and makes me super self-conscious, but once I got to know her she quickly dispelled any apprehension I had about her. "Nice work," she says as she tosses today's newspaper at me.

I flip the pages until I see my picture. An old building with peeling paint, broken windows, and a sagging front door sits just above the fold, accompanied by a story about the old gas station where teenagers have been hanging out. It's not the front page, but published is published.

When Mr. Turner, our photography teacher and the closest adult I had to a mentor, was arrested for kidnapping Cameron's sister and the other girls, Shelly came up with the idea for a work study for the best kids from our photography class. It's worked out pretty well since Stride Right didn't have a plan for when one of his beloved teachers was arrested. You'd have to torture me to get me to admit it, but I was thrilled to be among the eight students chosen. Those who weren't selected had to either switch to another elective or suffer through another hour of study hall, but none of them dream of someday being a professional photographer.

We've speculated about how old Shelly is—she doesn't look much older than us—but I haven't worked up the courage to ask her anything personal.

I sit at the end of the table as the front door opens and Cameron walks in. He catches my eye and mouths "sorry," then looks away as he joins us at the table.

Shelly nods at Cameron before turning her laptop to face us, revealing a photo of a fireman cradling a kitten to his chest.

I roll my eyes. Seriously? A kitten?

"What can you tell me about this picture?" Shelly always starts class with this question.

Several people answer at once.

"The fireman just rescued the kitten."

"The camera is practically resting on his shoulder."

"It was a slow news day." I can't help myself. Several people laugh but Shelly sets her mouth in a firm line. I hang my head. "Sorry."

"Biz may have a point, but there's something to be learned from even the most over-played images. The trick—" Shelly leans forward so she can see the screen "—is to find a unique way to present the information. This photographer could have taken the standard stand-five-feet-in-front-of-the-subject angle, but instead she shot over the fireman's shoulder, giving us a different perspective." She draws a line with her finger from the upper corner of the photo to the kitten's nose. "We see the kitten the way the fireman did... we're part of the shot rather than witnessing it."

My mind races. I've played around with perspective, but just by moving higher or lower to the subject. I hadn't considered turning the subject around. I glance at Cameron to see if he's as excited as I am, but he's focused on his phone in his lap.

Shelly closes her laptop and slides off the table. A smile lights her face. "Tomorrow I'd like you to bring in a few examples of a common image taken in a different perspective, then we'll start taking some of our own."

I can't help but smile back. When Turner was arrested I thought my brief fling with photography had come to an end, but Shelly has given me new hope. Kids at school may see me as a freak, but all of that slips away when I'm behind my camera. Its weight in my hands centers me, pulling me closer to the dance between light and shadows, allowing me to forget, if just for a moment, all the worries in my life and just be in the here and now.

Chapter 4

The house is quiet when I get home, which today turns out to be a good thing. Dad is reading a magazine on the couch. His light brown hair hangs limply against his forehead, his khakis and long-sleeved T-shirt loose on his frame.

I settle on the opposite end, backpack at my feet.

"Homework already?"

I shrug. "May as well get started. I don't want to bother you while you're reading."

"This?" He tosses what turns out to be a brochure, not a magazine. A brochure with four ethnically-diverse teenagers laughing on the cover, backpacks slung casually over shoulders, tall leafy trees in the background. "This is for you."

A flurry of emotions rattle through me. I've always figured I'd go to college—at my school it's assumed you'll go, even if it's just community college—but everyone applied while I was recovering from surgery, and then since Dad's gotten sicker I sort of without telling anyone decided that maybe I better stay home. I don't realize I'm clutching the brochure in my fist until Dad leans over and places his hand over mine.

"Hey, if you don't like this school we can look at others. They have a good photography program and I thought it was worth checking out."

I drop my head. "It's not that."

"Then what?"

How do I tell him that I don't want to move away when he keeps getting sicker?

"Biz, tell me what's going on."

I turn my hand over and squeeze his. I clear my throat. "What if you get sicker, if something really bad happens, and I'm off at college? I couldn't live with myself if I wasn't here for you." Now that I've said it out loud it doesn't sound as ridiculous as I thought. Surely he'll understand why—

"Biz, if you think I'm going to let you put your life on hold until…" he trails off, looking down at himself with disgust. "Until my body finally gives up on me, then you really don't know me at all. All I have left is making sure you get the life you deserve. We may not be able to send you to a fancy private college, but we'll send you somewhere."

I smile softly. "Can't wait to get rid of me, huh?"

He shakes his head, a smile brightening his eyes. "Hardly." He squeezes my hand again. "We want what's best for you and I don't think it's staying in this house for the rest of your life. There's a lot of world out there and you have a talent that can really take you places."

Everything he's saying makes sense, and deep down I agree with him, but I can't stop the wall that slams against my chest, urging me to resist, to blow it off like it doesn't matter. "Is this where we sing Kumbaya? Or am I buying the world a Coke?"

"Biz, stop. I know you can't take a compliment, but I'm trying to be serious. Photography can be a career for you—if you don't chase it away."

The smile drops from my face. He's right, I know he's right, but thinking about the future always sends me into a panic. I've managed to keep flickering a secret, but what if moving away triggers something that changes me from everyday freak to full-blown outcast? At least here I'm safe.

He reaches under his leg opposite me and pulls out a newspaper. He's a regular Houdini over there. "Besides, your actions speak louder than your words." He tosses a newspaper in my lap. It's the same one Shelly gave me earlier. "You can protest all you want, but you know I'm right."

A sigh escapes me. "Maybe." I unfold the paper and take my time flipping to my photo. I scan the article about the gas station, but my eyes keep bouncing back to the byline: Biz Clement. I hate when he's right.

Dad leans across the couch and pats my knee. "Mom and I will survive without you in the house. We'll miss you more than you can possibly understand, but I think it'd be good for you to see more of the world, get out there..."

I skim a story on the opposite page. A car jumped the curb and smashed through the front window of a coffee shop in the downtown district near the river. The driver was taken to the hospital—I can't help but wonder if Martinez happened to be driving the ambulance, like when we first met—along with two women who were hurt inside the shop. Scary, sure, but what really catches my attention is the fact that there isn't a picture to go along with the story.

A thought niggles at the edge of my mind.

Could I?

I already know the answer to that. After the surgery I promised I wouldn't flicker anymore, and except for a couple times when I wasn't paying attention when Cameron was driving, I haven't. And this would be cheating, another thing I promised I wouldn't do anymore. Dad is the only person who knows the truth about that one, and I really do want him to be proud of me.

I run the tip of my finger over the corner of the paper. Doing the right thing is easy. I just won't get up early. I'll go to school like every other day since the surgery and that will be that. No one would even know I considered cheating.

But... a picture of the crash would land me on the front page. If I do go to college, I'll need more than just silly pictures of benches and the high school football team in my portfolio. I'll need something newsworthy, something that shows my potential.

And no one would ever know how I got it.

*****

A gentle vibration under my head wakes me at 5:30am. I don't dare use the alarm when I'm sneaking out in the morning. Mom doesn't know about the flickering, but Dad does, so it's better that they stay asleep and find my note when they wake up in an hour.

When I'm already back to yesterday.

I grab an apple from the bowl on the counter but stop short before running out the door. Dad's pill bowl sits empty, staring at me. My eyes roll at the inanimate object that elicits far more emotion from me than is really healthy. Most days I can keep my concern for Dad at a distance, but moments like these, when I'm forced to face his illness head-on, the facade cracks ever so slightly.

I set my bag on the counter, open the cupboard with Dad's medicine, and count out his morning pills, setting them carefully in the little bowl. Task completed, I slip out the door.

A gentle fog greets me as I hurry down the driveway. Guilt tugs at my chest as I get into the car and roll backward down the driveway, but I bury it with a bite of apple. It's just this one time.

The Strand—my go-to place when I want to flicker—is only a couple miles from home and within minutes I'm rounding the bend, accelerating as the road straightens between the tall stretch of trees. I press the button to roll down my window. Having it up or down doesn't make a difference, but the crisp morning air feels good on my skin. Guilt, no matter how hard I try to argue it away, is making me sweat.

I can almost feel my dark curls whipping around my neck as the sun peeks through the trees. Not anymore. I press the gas harder. The sunlight starts to flicker and like a long-lost friend the tips of my fingers start to tingle. For the briefest moment a lump blocks my throat. After the surgery I thought I'd lost the ability to flicker—Martinez told me he'd fixed me when he removed the mass from my brain, even though he still doesn't know what he was truly dealing with—and I tried to accept being normal, but it took less than a month to learn that I would never be normal. The difference is now I'm okay with that.

The tingling zips through my body to my toes, then the crushing weight descends, pushing, pushing me down into the seat. My fingers struggle to keep their grip on the steering wheel until—finally!—the weight lifts and I'm shooting through the ceiling. Well, not literally, but before I can catch my breath—

—I'm jerking awake at the kitchen table.

Dad raises an eyebrow but doesn't say anything. He knows.

Chapter 5

I breeze through the day on auto-pilot—if you count checking my watch every ten minutes to see if it's lunchtime yet breezing. When the lunch bell finally rings I weave against the flow of bodies swarming toward the cafeteria, finally stopping at my locker. The article said the accident happened at the tail end of the lunch rush, which means I have over an hour to get there since high school has lunch so fricking early.

As I hurry through the now-deserted hallway, a figure at the end of one of the smaller halls catches my attention. I pause for a half-step and my heart leaps. The boy is talking on his cell, hunched over with his head tilted toward a locker, but I'd know that body anywhere. He runs his fingers through his shaggy hair while he talks, oblivious that he's being watched. A soft smile spreads over his face and I lift my hand to wave but his gaze never reaches me. He's smiling at whoever he's talking to.

The smile that's supposed to be just for me.

A dagger slides through my heart and I force my feet to move away before he notices me. If the look on my face is anything like the anger and jealousy and hurt that's coursing through me, I don't want him to see it. One name repeats through my head. He swears they're just friends who are helping each other through a really hard time, that no one else could possibly understand the misery they've been through and the pieces they were left to pick up. How am I supposed to compete with that?

I pause around the corner and press my forehead against the wall. My heart feels too big for my chest. My empty stomach twists into a knot. Maybe it's all in my head. Maybe the part of my brain that is learning to frame every situation into a possible photo captured something that wasn't there. If I could just see him for a second more...

I lean toward the corner, desperation preparing me to see Cameron laughing, or standing with his shoulders relaxed, hand in his pocket, anything but the secretive pose I saw a moment earlier. A door bursts open behind me, snapping me out of my teen-drama moment. With a shake of my head, I adjust my bag on my shoulder and hustle down the hall to the parking lot. If I want to get this shot, I can't waste time worrying about Cameron and Sarah.

The sun sits high in the sky—good thing because flickering while inside a flicker would be beyond bad. The last time I did it I ended up in the hospital with my fabulous new haircut. Catching Turner and helping the kidnapped girls get home was worth it; getting a photo in the local paper is trivial in comparison.

I push my sunglasses tighter against my face and drive toward downtown, paying extra attention to traffic. Getting in an accident right when I got my driving privileges back would also not be good. The coffee shop where the accident happened is in a part of town I don't normally visit. Teenagers stick to the mall and fast food restaurants closer to school; the district near the river full of boutiques and coffee houses and strange little shops full of cheese and olive oil is unofficially off-limits.

Cars fill the parking lot next to the coffee shop and the

sunny day has brought the worker-bees out in full force. I ease down the street, my plan still developing. I don't want to sit in the shop where the car will hit—Dad might kill me if I end up in the hospital again—but lingering on the street might draw attention. I swing the car into a spot two blocks away, grab my camera, and beeline for a deli across the street from the coffee shop. The last thing I need is to end up with a head full of glass. Gashes and a shaved head are not the look I'm going for.

A bell tinkles against the glass door as I push my way inside. A group of men in business suits glance in my direction, but no one else pays much attention to the only teenager in the restaurant. My gaze jumps back and forth from the couple in line in front of me to the shop across the street. The accident isn't supposed to happen for another half hour but I'll be pissed if I miss it because people can't decide what they want. My gaze lingers on a pair of women sitting on a bench outside. They could be the people who were hurt. Maybe I should warn them instead of thinking about myself. But what would I—

"Miss, what can I get you?"

My head whips to the cashier. Warmth floods my cheeks. Now I'm the person holding up the line. "Sorry. Turkey on wheat and a bottle of water. Oh, and an apple if you've got it." Better prep for the headache now. I don't have actual proof, but I read somewhere that apples help stave off migraines and I'll take any advantage I can get. Besides, it's not like they're bad for me.

A few minutes later I'm back outside, camera balanced on my knees, the paper bag next to me on a low wall surrounding a planter box. Rubbing the apple against my shirt, I can't stop my mind from drifting to Cameron and the smile in the hallway.

I don't want to be jealous.

I don't want to be jealous.

I don't want to be jealous.

I toss the apple in the bag with my sandwich. Who else could he be talking to but Sarah? His mom sure as hell doesn't get that kind of a smile out of him. Katie? Maybe... I groan. If the knot in my stomach had arms it'd reach up and smack me in the face for being such a girl, but I can't help it. Not when it comes to Cameron. If I lose him now I'm losing more than just a boyfriend—I'm losing one of my best friends, too.

My phone sits silent in my pocket. No text from him asking why I'm not at lunch. My fingers reach for the phone and tug it out of my pocket, ignoring my inner voice yelling "Stop it!" I'm about to press his number when the sound of squealing tires echoes down the street. I'm on my feet before I have time to think, camera pressed to my face, as a silver sedan crashes into the front of the coffee shop. Click-click-click.

Everything moves in slow motion. People running, cars screeching to a stop, and the delicate tinkle of glass bouncing across the sidewalk. I rush into the street—look right, then left, then right again—my finger never leaving the shutter release. The driver is leaning against the steering wheel, her arms bent in a way that seems unnatural, while two women lay motionless in front of the car, their bodies tossed from their chairs like discarded toys. I stop at the edge of the road, not sure what to do. A man from inside the coffee shop rushes to the woman nearest to me. Kneeling next to her, he adjusts her skirt so it covers her upper thighs. Click-click-click. He glances at me for half a heartbeat, his hands moving over her arms, her side, her throat. A low moan sounds from the other woman, quickly drowned out by the distant wail of sirens.

My phone vibrates in my pocket but I ignore it. Cameron can wait.

The second woman lifts her head and I gasp. Blood covers her face, running from a gash somewhere in her hair, dripping off her nose and chin, splattering the pavement beneath her. Click-click-click.

I should help. This isn't like the accident I photographed last spring when I got in the paper for the first time. Then the police were already there. Here it's just people who were eating lunch or happened to be walking by. I sling my camera over my shoulder and take a tentative step toward the woman when a man in an EMT uniform brushes past me.

"Excuse me, miss." His attention never leaves the woman.

I stumble back until my feet hit the low wall of another planter. Maybe I'm better here, out of the way.

The EMTs work on the two women and within minutes have the driver out of the car and on a stretcher, her arms strapped over her chest and a neck brace stabilizing her head.

Click-click-click.

Lights from the ambulance bounce off the brick, freezing me for a half second. I blink it away. These lights can't affect me. Well, they can still make my body react—that's what happened the first time I met Martinez—but I won't flicker. Artificial light gives me the fun side effects without the headache: I tingle, get light-headed, and my pupils go all wonky, but I'm stuck in the present if I make a scene. At least with flickering, no one remembers when I momentarily lose control of myself.

I zoom in on the faces of the people standing on the opposite side of the crowd, focusing in on a guy not much older than me. His hand covers his mouth, and his eyes show a mixture of horror and excitement. I turn away in disgust, then a realization hits me: what if I have that same look on my face? Part of being a photographer is that you're in the right place at the right time and getting in the middle of the action, even when it makes your stomach turn, but what if people think I'm happy there's an accident?

I take a few steps back, the rush of adrenaline fading. For the first time since the car crashed into the women, I really see the scene in front of me: mangled bodies covered in broken glass, discarded paper napkins dancing lightly over the sidewalk, unaware of the mayhem swirling around them. The weight of my camera is suddenly unbearable and I slump onto one of the concrete planters.

Did I do the right thing by flickering?

Photographers make their living taking pictures of all kinds of things, most of which never put them or other people in danger, but if I want to be a real photojournalist, I need to get over the fear that rather than helping, I'm adding to the problem. Rushing from one catastrophe to the next and climbing into the middle of the chaos is part of the job.

I take a slow breath. Can I really do this for the rest of my life?

Chapter 6

I yank on the glass door to the Chronicle, ignoring the disapproving shouts inside my head. Yes, I know I should go back to class, but what was the point of skipping if I don't turn in the photos? Shelly isn't at her desk so I grab an empty envelope and drop my memory card inside. I scribble a note on the front:

Shots from an accident today.

I'll text details.

Biz.

No one pays any attention to me, but I can't shake the

feeling that I'm doing something wrong. Technically this is for photography class so technically I just took a field trip. A solo, unapproved field trip. Maybe I should get a note.

A guy on the other side of the room makes me catch my breath. Dark hair, long-sleeved t-shirt with the sleeves pushed over his elbows. Before I can stop it my heart flutters and a smile spreads over my face, but he turns in my direction and my stomach drops. It's not Cameron. The guy nods at me then turns back around. I'll ask someone else for the note.

*****

Chocolate shakes really are nature's miracle. They're refreshing, delicious, and cure any ailment known to man, including a not-quite broken heart but one that is decidedly bruised. Settled on a park bench around the corner from the newspaper, I had planned to go back to school, but when the grandmotherly woman who writes obituaries wrote the time on my note I realized I only had half an hour before I had to be back here for class. Besides, a little chocolate therapy sounded much better than Trig.

I take another sip and stare at my phone, unsure what to do

about Cameron. The text earlier was Amelia, not him. Until today I'd assumed this was all in my head and that he was just having a hard time with Katie, but now everything's been flipped upside down. Amelia might be able to help—she's much better at the dating thing, at least when it comes to getting guys to stick around. Until Cameron I'd always pushed them away before they could truly figure me out.

I pull up Amelia's number.

> Me: Can you come over later? Cam issues...

She writes back almost immediately.

> Amelia: Yes. Where are you? I missed you at lunch. xoxo

Crap. I was so worried about Cameron I forget to tell Amelia I wouldn't be there.

> Me: Taking pictures. I'll explain later.

Before long, kids from class arrive one by one, and one by one they give me a puzzled look as they walk by and I don't get up to join them. I don't budge until I see Old Berta, Cameron's hideous orange car, roll into a parking spot across the street. Grateful for the weight of my camera over my shoulder, I rub my fingernails over the coarse stitching of the strap until he notices me waiting.

A broad smile stretches over his face. "Biz, hey!" He closes the space between us and before I can say a word he wraps his arms around me and plants a kiss firmly on my lips. "I feel like I haven't talked to you in forever."

What the eff? "Yeah, me too." I slide my arms around his narrow waist but don't pull him as close as normal. I love nothing more than the feel of his chest pressed against mine, but a smile and a kiss—albeit a very nice kiss—aren't enough to erase the turmoil I feel.

He notices my hesitation and pulls back to look me in the eyes. "What's wrong?"

I shake my head. Where do I begin? I've become the neurotic, jealous girlfriend I despise.

He kisses my forehead. "I'm sorry I missed you at lunch."

He didn't even notice I wasn't there? Well I guess that explains why he didn't text.

"I called Sarah to tell her about Katie's latest BS and we talked longer than I meant to."

That doesn't make me feel better. "What's going on with Katie?"

His arms drop to his sides as he exhales. It's like he's deflating right in front of me. "She skipped class three times this week. Mom's worried about some new friends she's hanging out with but I keep telling her she's being overprotective."

"Can you blame her?"

He gives me a hurt look.

"Sorry, I just mean... I'm sure Katie's got a lot of mixed up feelings right now and the kids she was friends with four years ago may not understand what she's dealing with. We don't even understand." His sad eyes never leave mine. It's unsettling. I take a deep breath and ask what I don't want to. "What did Sarah say?"

Is it my imagination or do his eyes light up when I say her name?

"Her sister is skipping, too."

"Are they hanging out together?"

"We don't know. I would guess yes. I'm going to ask Katie about it tonight." He runs a hand through the hair that brushes his eyes. "I feel like I need to protect her, to keep something bad from happening. Again."

I reach up and cradle his face with my hands. "Cam, it's not your fault she got taken."

He looks away, but not before I notice the tears in his eyes.

"I was supposed to be watching her. I should have gone with her to the front yard."

"You were barely older than she is now. You can't keep beating yourself up over this." I'll never forget the panic in Cameron's voice when he called to tell me that Katie had disappeared. I rode my bike to his house as fast as I could—later we told the police that I'd been there when it happened—but it was too late. He's blamed himself ever since.

He pulls away. Straightens his shoulders. "I can because it's true. But I'm not going to let anything happen to her again. Sarah said—"

I roll my eyes. I can't help it. Why does everything have to go back to her?

"What?" The tears are gone, replaced by a glare I've rarely seen directed at me.

"Nothing."

"No, not nothing." He raises his hand and I flinch, but he rests it gently on my arm, the anger gone as fast as it arrived. "Biz, what's going on?"

"It's just..." I look away, unable to look him in the eye. I've always prided myself on being rational, and I'm afraid that if he sees how jealous I am, that I've changed from his best friend to another silly girl, he might decide I'm not worth the effort.

"Tell me."

Heat rushes to my cheeks. "It's Sarah. I guess I'm a little jealous of her, of this connection you two have." It sounds even worse out loud. Rationally, I know it makes sense for him to talk to Sarah because her family is going through the same thing, but that logic is no match for the knot in my stomach. "I know it's stupid."

"Biz, I told you. We're just friends." He slides his hand down my arm until his fingers lace through mine. "Yeah, Sarah understands what I'm going through with Katie but that doesn't mean I like her. We're like a support group for each other."

"Okay. I'm sorry I keep questioning it." I want to believe him, and based on the flutters in my stomach my gut already does, but I still can't kick the suspicion that there's more to their friendship than he's letting on.

He tugs my hand. "We better get inside before we miss the entire class."

We're greeted with several whistles from the back of the room. "Nice of you to join us," Shelly calls over the head of the real workers, so now every person in the room is staring at us. I don't think Shelly's upset. For her, embarrassing us is enough punishment for being late to class.

The only empty seats are on opposite ends of the group. As I drop my bag on the floor, Shelly calls my name.

"Biz, nice work with the accident. It's too late to get them into today's paper, but they'll be front page tomorrow." Her smile lights up her eyes and I feel embarrassed for the second time since I got here. But this feeling is different. My heart swells with an unfamiliar pressure and I can't stop the smile that tugs at my lips. I can deal with this kind of embarrassment.

Cameron leans back in his seat so we can see each other behind the kids between us. He raises his eyebrows and opens his hands as if to say "what?" I was so worked up about Sarah I forgot to tell him about the accident.

I mouth "I'll tell you later" then sit forward. I want to enjoy this moment. Everyone in class has had something printed in the paper, but the front page is hard to get even for the staff photographers. I can already imagine it in my portfolio.

A small voice whispers in my head, "But they didn't cheat to get it."

Chapter 7

Amelia arrives with her backpack over one shoulder and a bag stuffed with chips, Twizzlers, and a two-liter of Coke in the other. "This sounds like a problem for junk food."

I jump into the doorway and hug her tightly, nearly knocking her over. "Thank you."

Amelia laughs. "Whoa, whoa, what's all this? I'm the one who tackles people when they aren't expecting it." She pushes past me toward the kitchen, where she sets the snacks next to today's newspaper. The one with my pictures of the gas station. "This is more serious than I thought."

Dad is upstairs taking a nap but I glance up the stairway to make sure his door is shut before dumping the whole story about Cameron on her. "He insists they're just friends, but if you'd seen the look on his face when he was on the phone..."

Amelia chews a Twizzler thoughtfully. "Do you know for sure it was Support Group Sarah on the phone?"

"No, but who else could it be?"

She sits quietly for another beat, then points the Twizzler at me. "We need to get them in the same room!"

My stomach turns. "How is that supposed to help?"

"I don't mean to set them up, goofy, I mean to see how they act together. If they act normal then you know nothing's going on. If they're all touchy-feely, then you... welllll..." Her excitement fades. "Then at least you know."

"Yeah." Playing games goes against everything inside me, but I don't know another way to figure out the truth. "So how do we get them together?"

Amelia smiles weakly. "A party?"

"Seriously?"

"This could work." She leans a hip against the counter, hands ready to orchestrate her idea. "You never had a hey-I-made-it-out-of-surgery party." She catches my rolled eyes and holds up a hand, palm facing me. "Biz, you know you're dying to let everyone see your scalp up close."

I laugh. "Sure, but a party?"

"What if I promise there will be no dancing?"

"And no disco balls?"

"You and the sparkly lights." She sighs dramatically, shoulders rising and falling, and draws a horizontal line in the air, crossing it off the list. "Fine, no disco balls."

"So how do we get Sarah there? It's not like she's friends with us."

"What about Katie? We could make it a yay-surgery's-over slash welcome-home-kidnapped-girls party."

I throw a Twizzler at her head. "That's morbid. And isn't she a little young to be hanging out with our friends?"

She shrugs. "People have little brothers and sisters. We'll just put them at a kids table."

"I guess." I can't help but think of the last party I was at with Katie. It was her seventh birthday, just a few months before she was kidnapped. Back then she wore pigtails and a smile wherever she went, but aside from the occasional smirk, I can't say I've seen either since she's been home.

"It'll work. We just need to work on the tagline." She takes a bite of the Twizzler that I threw at her and leans her elbows on the counter. "There is one other thing we could celebrate."

"Oh yeah?" It's not like Amelia to keep secrets from me.

She reaches into her backpack and tosses a thick envelope at me. "I got in!"

I yank the letter from the envelope and read, "...pleased to inform you that we have accepted your application for..." I toss the letter aside and scramble around the island to hug her. "Amelia, that's fantastic!"

I've never seen her smile bigger. "I know! All that stress over Trig and I got early admission anyway." Her smile fades. "Have you decided what you want to do? You still have time to apply, right?"

I sit on the closest stool. "I think so." Part of me is jealous that Amelia seems to have college, and pretty much her entire future, figured out. Sometimes I wish I could focus on nothing more than photography and college, but I'm stuck in a circle worrying about Katie, Dad, and what flickering will do to me later in life. "I've always assumed I'll go to college, but with my dad, I don't know how I can move away."

"Have you talked to him about it?"

The corner of my mouth lifts. "He's been sending away for brochures."

She bounces on her feet. "Come to State with me!"

Amelia makes it sound so easy. Just fill out an application and write a couple essays, then boom, you're a college student. "Will it make you happy if I promise to consider it?"

She smiles. "Yes. Now, will your parents let you have a party?"

I've never had more than two or three friends over at one time. The fear of Dad having a seizure is never far from my thoughts and while people know he's sick, it's an entirely different thing to see it in action. I take a deep breath and smile at Amelia. "There's a first time for everything."

We settle at the dining table to do homework until Dad wakes up, which surprisingly doesn't happen until Mom gets home from work. It's not like him to stay asleep once I get home from school. I watch Mom carefully as she enters the kitchen, searching for a sign that she's hiding something from me. Her shoulders slump a little more than normal and a few pieces of hair have loosened from her bun, but I can't say that's different from any other day. "Hey, Mom."

"Hi, girls." Her eyes light up when she sees us and she smiles at our books scattered across the table. She glances into the living room. "Is your dad resting?"

"Yeah, he went up there when I got home."

She hangs her purse on the back of a chair and steps lightly up the stairs. Low voices drift down to us.

"Is your dad okay?" Aside from Cameron, who knows the truth about Dad, Amelia knows more about Dad's illness than anyone outside my family. She's been here for a seizure and kept me company during some of his hospital visits, but I don't like to talk about that part of him.

"I'm not sure. Usually he stays up when I get home from school." And I was so self-absorbed I never stopped to wonder if he needed my help. How much aren't they telling me? What if they think I don't care? I close my eyes and make a silent promise to pay more attention to how he's doing, rather than waiting for them to tell me.

The stairs creak and Amelia looks past me. "Hey, Mr. Biz."

I can feel Dad smile behind me. He's always had a soft spot for my best friend and her nickname for him always lightens his mood.

"Hi, Amelia. Biz." He rests a hand on my shoulder and kisses the top of my head.

I grab his hand. "Can I get you anything?" I face Mom. "Do you need me to help with dinner?"

Dad laughs. "If I didn't know better I'd think you want something."

Amelia snorts as I stutter a protest. "No... I... I just want to help! Really."

Amelia kicks me under the table.

"Okay, I guess there is one thing I wanted to ask you."

Mom reaches into the cabinet and starts filling the pill bowl with Dad's evening doses. She raises an eyebrow. "This ought to be good."

Amelia sits up straight, smiling. "It is."

"So let's hear it." Dad squeezes my shoulder.

I look back and forth between them. "I was wondering if maybe I could have a party. To celebrate the whole surviving brain surgery thing and the fact that I'm not a vegetable." I try not to think about that side of the surgery but it's true: one wrong slip of Martinez's scalpel and I wouldn't even know to worry about my shaved head.

Mom has a funny look on her face. Maybe I pushed it too far. Her smile is a little wobbly and her eyes are tighter than normal.

I reach for her hand, and her fingers tighten around mine. "Are you okay? I didn't mean to sound so callous." I mentally smack myself. My parents were so supportive through my surgery and recovery that I forget how scary it must have been for them. No one wants to see their daughter's head cracked open.

Mom gives my hand a final squeeze before letting go. "I think a party is a good idea. You should celebrate." She carries the pill bowl and a glass of water to the table and sets it down in front of Dad. "When were you thinking?"

I glance at Amelia. We hadn't gotten that far in our planning. Soon. "Next Friday?"

Dad coughs behind me. "Works for me."

Amelia's head bobs up and down and she swats my arm. "Time to get planning!"

We gather our books and hurry upstairs before either of them can change their mind. My phone is out before Amelia settles on the bed.

"Texting Cam?"

"Yeah."

"So how are you going to get him to invite Sarah? Don't you think that'll seem a little weird?"

I sit on floor and lean against the side of the bed, waiting for Cam to text back. "I'll just tell him I feel bad for doubting him and want to get to know her better." I pick at the corner of the bedspread. "It's the truth. I do feel bad for doubting him."

"Cam isn't the type to do something behind your back."

I know she's right, but that doesn't change the nerves fluttering through me. Something is off with us.

My phone dings in my hand. Amelia leans forward, eyebrows raised. "He says 'sounds fun'. What is it with guys and their short messages?"

Amelia throws a pillow at my head. "Would you stop? Tell him to invite Sarah."

My fingers fly over the keyboard. "Give me a minute."

Me: How's it going?

Cameron: Okay. Worried about Katie.

Me: Did something happen?

Cameron: Nothing new. Mom doesn't like her friends.

Me: What if you invite them to my party?

Cameron: You sure?

Me: Then we can check them out. Smack 'em around if they're trouble.

Cameron: LOL

Me: Seriously.

"What's he saying?" Amelia leans over my shoulder.

"Give me a sec. I'm about to tell him to invite Sarah." It's not like Cameron can see me, but I take a deep breath anyway.

Me: What if you invite Sarah and her sister?

"Okay, I asked."

"Why is he taking so long to write back?"

"It's been two seconds." My phone dings and Amelia leans her head against mine.

Cameron: You sure?

I look at Amelia.

She nods at my phone. "Y-E-S."

Me: Yes.

Cameron: I'll ask her.

My stomach twists. I know this is what we planned, but I hate the idea of them talking, texting, emailing, whatever. "I don't know if I can do this."

"Since when are you the jealous type?"

She's right. This isn't like me and these unfamiliar feelings have my head all out of sorts. Usually I'm the one ditching a guy as soon as he gets too needy. But this is different. I close my eyes. "Since I started dating Cam. And Katie..." I shake my head. "I feel responsible for her. I can't turn my back on her now."

Chapter 8

The alarm shoots needles through my eyeballs before I'm ready. I took a migraine pill before bed but it helps about as much as rubbing a kitten on my face. A quick smack on the phone stops the beeping, but does nothing for my head. With a shaky sigh I roll out of bed and onto the floor so I'm on my hands and knees.

"You can do this." This is the bad part of flickering. Sure, going back and repeating things—or like yesterday, discovering new things to do—is great, but the fun lessons I've learned over the years is there's always a consequence. I used to stay home with every headache but I came precariously close to getting held back a grade and decided that struggling through school is the price I must pay for flickering. But before I can do that, I need to get past Mom. If she sees me like this she won't let me leave.

I wiggle into jeans and a sweatshirt from the floor. Shoes, I need shoes. I scan the room with half-closed eyes. Sneakers are by the door. Done. Part of the reason I have to sneak past Mom is there's no hiding how I feel when I'm dressed like a homeless person. At least no one at school says anything anymore.

A sliver of light beneath my parents' bedroom door shouts hello, so I slip into the bathroom, do a minimal amount of beautifying—brush teeth, splash water on face—then tiptoe downstairs.

Once outside I put the car in neutral and roll into the street before starting the engine. Only then do I let out the breath I've been holding.

School is school. Boring lectures, loud students, and freakishly bright lights. I dream of the day they ditch the flucrescent lights and bring in a few old-school 60-watt bulbs, or allow me to wear sunglasses. But that would draw even more attention to myself and then the school nurse, Becky, will swoop in and call my mom. Nope, I'll deal with the lights.

My head is buried deep in my locker under the pretense of looking for a book—really I'm closing my eyes for a second—when strong hands wrap around my waist. I jump, slamming my head into the side of the locker, then fall to my knees. "What the hell?"

The hands pull me to my feet and engulf me in a warm, snuggly hug. Cameron laughs softly in my ear. "That wasn't the reaction I was hoping for."

I bury my face in his chest and breathe deeply. "I've missed you." His smell, his voice, the feel of him pressed close to me. My worries about Sarah melt away.

He brushes his fingers over my forehead, trailing them down my cheek until they slide around the base of my neck. For a moment I have a pang of regret that he can't run his fingers through my hair anymore, but I push it away. I need this. His head lowers and I take a quick breath as his mouth covers mine. There's a no-kissing policy at school, but surely there's an exception when your boyfriend is as hot as mine.

An elbow jabs me in the side and I knock teeth with Cameron.

"Freak." A freshman in all black with chains dripping from

his waist smirks over his shoulder as he continues down the hall with two girls in equally colorful outfits and way too much eye makeup.

Cameron turns to follow but I grab his arm. "Cam, don't."

He crosses and uncrosses his arms, flexing his hands, before finally resting them on my arms. "Has he bothered you before?"

I look at the kid's back halfway down the hall. "Him? No."

"But others have?"

I shrug, resisting the urge to touch my hair. Unfortunately for me, high school places a lot of importance on looks. Before my surgery I fell into the looks-normal-enough-to-blend-in crowd, but not anymore. "What can I say? He's right."

"That goth wannabe loser? He doesn't even know you."

"He knows enough to know I'm a freak."

Cameron pulls me back to his chest. "You're not. Yeah, you're different, and the flickering thing is a bit weird, but that doesn't mean—"

"Cam, it's okay."

"—that doesn't mean people can touch you. What happened to bullying by just calling names?"

I think of the two girls walking with him. "He's probably

just showing off for those girls. Seriously, forget about it." I touch his cheek with my fingers, coaxing him toward me for another kiss just as the bell rings. I pull away. "I'll see you at lunch."

The day-after-flickering headaches make it nearly impossible to concentrate, but after getting accused of cheating a few months ago I've tried to make more of an effort. True, I was cheating, but it was usually a side effect of flickering for something else, like my first date with Cameron, and retaking the test was just a bonus. I don't have any tests today but I swear a couple teachers have given me the stink-eye.

At lunch I grab an apple and a granola bar before weaving my way to the empty table I share with Amelia and Cameron. Grateful for a few moments of quiet—if you can have quiet in a high school cafeteria. I mean, it's like they add noise-enhancing panels in the ceiling that reverberate every sound wave straight into my skull—I rest my head face down on my folded arms until Amelia's sing-songy voice drifts my way. She's not alone.

"This means I don't have to study any more!"

"Can't they take away their acceptance if you bomb senior year?" asks a male voice.

"Whatever. I'm totally in and I'm not worrying about Trig anymore."

I lift my head and nod at Trace, Amelia's soccer-playing boyfriend, before giving her a grateful smile. He splits his time between us and the soccer team, and she must have asked him to join us today since she knew I'd be useless for conversation.

"Hey, Biz. Another headache?" She squeezes the back of my neck before sitting down across from me. Part of me yearns for her to keep rubbing, but that would be weird.

"Yeah."

"That sucks. Trace was just telling me about when he got a concussion last year. He went for a header and slammed his head into the side of the goal."

He nods, mouth full.

"He had to go the hospital and everything!"

"Did you score?"

He laughs. "Of course. But I didn't know until five minutes after. Knocked me out." He takes another bite. "Too bad you didn't get a picture of that. I would have made the paper for sure."

I roll my eyes as Amelia rubs his arm. Trace is pretty

well-rounded as far as jocks go, but every now and then he reminds me why I don't usually hang out with them. I need a little more conversation in my conversation.

"Hey, that reminds me," Amelia says. "Did your pictures from the accident make it into the paper?"

I'm reaching for my phone before she finishes her sentence. "I totally forgot. I don't know." The website is still loading when Cameron sets his tray next to me and looks over my shoulder, his cheek resting against mine.

"What are we looking up?"

I turn my face to give him a quick kiss on the cheek. "To see if I'm in the paper today."

He pulls out the chair and slides his lean body into the seat in one fluid motion, and for a moment I forget what we're talking about. "I checked during class. You are."

A rush of excitement zips through me. "Really?"

He smiles and my stomach does a little flip. "Yep. Front page." He leans closer and kisses me again. "Nice work."

The excitement fades. Work, right. Sure, I was there at the right time and took the pictures, but I flat-out cheated to get there. A knot of worry hardens in my chest. Just because I have the ability to go back doesn't mean I should, especially if it's not helping anyone but myself.

I plaster a smile on my face before Cameron notices my change in mood, but he's already distracted by his phone. He types quickly, hits send, and blacks out the screen before I can see who it is.

The three of them eat their lunches, laughing without me, and for the time being I'm grateful that my friends have gotten used to my bizarre ways because if anyone asks me what's wrong I might burst into tears.

Chapter 9

My day gets even better in Bishop's class. The odds of me using anything resembling Trig once I graduate from high school are about as good as me winning the national cheerleading championship, yet every day he drones on and on about sine and cosine and springs quizzes on us when I can't focus for more than a minute or two. When the bell rings at the end of class I slide my paper onto his desk and melt into the rest of the bodies fleeing to the hallway.

We're supposed to go straight to the Chronicle, but right now caffeine is more important than being on time so I head to the closest fast food place, a knock-off Taco Bell. The line of cars at the drive-through snakes all the way to the street, so I park and rush inside. I fling open the door and someone slams their shoulder into me, nearly knocking me over. "Hey!"

It's the same guy from earlier, but this time he doesn't hurry away. Instead he stands there, hands shoved in his black jeans, as if he's waiting to see how I'll react. The girls with him giggle. If I didn't have this damn headache I'd shove him back, but my energy level is hovering near slug.

I scowl. "What's your problem?"

He lifts one shoulder in a half shrug.

One of the girls—a different girl from earlier—shifts her bag on her shoulder. "Come on, Nate. Leave her alone."

A flash of recognition hits me. "Katie?" I barely recognize her. The clothes are the same as the last time I saw her, but now her black hair has a bluish tint and is cut short in back with long chunks hanging over her eyes.

Nate looks at Katie. "You know this freak?"

I cross my arms. "That's quite a compliment, coming from you." I give him a once over and a look that's supposed to be intimidating, but my heart's not in it. What the hell is Katie doing with this jerk?

"She's my brother's girlfriend."

"Don't forget that I've known you since you were three."

"Yeah, that too."

Nate scoffs. "Sucks to be you." He turns to walk away, hands still stuffed in his pockets. It's an awkward gait—slightly hunched over with wide steps, almost like he just got off a horse—but the girls trailing after him don't seem to notice.

Katie doesn't follow him.

"He seems nice."

She dips her head so her hair falls in her face. "He's not so bad."

"Right." There are so many things I want to say to her but with this new attitude I don't think she'd listen. I long for the days when I could just scoop her into my arms and tickle her until she spilled her secrets, but I don't think that'd go over real well. "So what are you doing here?"

"Getting food."

"Yeah, I realize that. I thought you were supposed to be with a tutor. At least while you get caught up."

She stiffens, a slight shift in posture that anyone else might not notice but that completely changes her demeanor, then a breath later relaxes her shoulders and lowers her bag to her hip. I knew this was hard for her but didn't realize how much effort every moment took. The Katie I know is still in there someplace. "I have tutors in the morning, but in the afternoon I'm in sixth grade with everyone else. I guess someone decided that after being locked in a room for four years they should probably let me be around other kids."

Her words hit me like a slap. She's never spoken so bluntly about her time with Turner. Images of the Katie from four years ago tumble together with the teacher I adored and I have to force myself to catch a breath.

She notices. "That's the same reaction my tutor had when I said I want to join the living." She jerks her head so her hair moves off her face and I notice a tiny stud in her nose. "It's a lot easier to sneak away from school than it was from one person. But if anyone asks, it was the school's idea to readapt me to normal life."

I jut my chin in Nate's direction. "He's considered normal?" I realize too late what I've said. Nate may be a jerk to me, but he makes Katie feel accepted and I've just crapped all over that.

She crosses her arms, daring me to continue.

Mentioning the party now seems stupid, but I have to try.

"So, I'm having a party next week if you want to come."

She starts to say something, then seems to change her mind. A smirk replaces the scowl from a moment before. "Can I bring Nate? Or is it just for normal people?"

I had that coming. "Only if he promises to stay away from me."

A sound bubbles from her throat, the closest thing to a laugh I've heard from her. For a second we're in her backyard and I'm pushing her on the swings, her laughter growing louder with each pass. It seems ridiculous to think that anything I do can bring back that little girl, but I can't help but hope for it.

I shake my head to clear my thoughts. "Sure, why not."

Nate shouts from a table near the front windows. "Katie, you coming?"

She flinches, a slight tremor in her eyes, but shakes it off.

I narrow my focus on Nate. I figured he's all talk, but he pushed me for no reason. What if he's done that to Katie? I try to catch her eye but she won't look at me. "See you later."

She takes a deep breath and straightens her shoulders. "Yeah, whatever." Mask back on, she leaves me to join her friends.

*****

Nerves hit me when I'm driving to the Chronicle. I've been in the paper before but this time it's different. This isn't the first time I flickered so I could cheat, but this feels bigger than a silly Trig test. Shelly's ready for me when I arrive at the paper, waving from across the room as soon as I step inside.

"Biz!" She holds up the paper. "Nice work!"

All but one of the kids already sitting at the table turn to look at me and I falter for a second, heat already rising in my cheeks. Even though I expected this, I don't like being at the center of attention. That's why I hide behind the camera. But this is different. I feel like the word CHEATER is bouncing over my head in neon lights, with a blinking arrow pointing at my forehead.

I force a smile. "Thanks."

She slides the paper across the table, pictures of the crash at the coffee shop coming to a rest upside down. I spin it around and my eye goes straight to my byline. Biz Clement. Okay, that kills some of the nerves. Even though Cameron told me they were published, I never believe it until I see my name with my own eyes.

Shelly waits until everyone arrives to speak. "Three of you were published in the paper yesterday. Hannah, with her photo of a group of kids playing kickball that ran with a feature story on health, and Ethan's shot of two puppies playing in the leaves was the photo of the week."

The class applauds politely and Hannah and Ethan both smile.

"And of course we have Biz, who managed to be across the street from a coffee shop when a car crashed into the building." She holds up a second copy of the paper. The largest picture is of the EMT working on one of the women who was hit by the car. His clenched jaw and the taut muscles in his arms bring me back to that moment and a wave of nausea passes through me. I swallow hard, forcing down the sharp taste of bile.

The girl on my right smiles at me. "You're so lucky you were there. Why were you even downtown at lunch?"

My mouth opens but nothing comes out. A smart person would have prepared an answer, especially since I knew they'd been published hours earlier. I wipe the sweat that's formed above my lip. "Have you ever been to Fortinos? Their shakes are to die for."

She narrows her eyes. "Seems like a long way to go for a shake."

I shrug. "You clearly haven't tried one."

She turns away and I wrap my arms around my belly. I've learned to deal with the headaches after flickering, but the guilt is new. Cheating isn't worth this.

I try to pay attention during the rest of class, but struggling with this headache all day has completely wiped me out. It's all I can do to keep my head up and my eyes open.

Cameron drapes an arm around my shoulder as we leave. "Bad day?"

I nod into his shoulder.

"Would a shake from Fortinos help?"

I nod harder, closing an eye. I can see where we're going with one.

He lowers his arm and slips his fingers through mine. "Anything special, or just the headache?"

"Mostly the headache. I ran into that goth-wannabe guy earlier."

His fingers tighten over mine. "Did he touch you again?"

"No, but guess who was with him this time." I glance up

at him then quickly look back down when the sun scalds my eyeballs.

"I give up."

I take a breath. "Katie."

He stops walking. "My sister." His voice is low, threatening, and it's not a question. His shoulders straighten.

I haven't seen this Cameron in a really long time. Not since people found out he was questioned after Katie disappeared.

"Was she with-him with him?"

I put a hand on his chest. "No! At least it didn't seem like it. I ran into her when I stopped to get some caffeine. She was with him and a couple other girls." I think back, trying to recall some detail to assure Cameron that his baby sister isn't crushing on a delinquent. "But I did invite them to my party."

He opens his mouth but I press harder on his chest to stop him. "I know, I don't exactly want him there either. She promised Nate would leave me alone. But look at the plus side, now we can see how she is with her friends. Find out how she's really doing."

Cameron's body relaxes. "You have a point. But I swear I'll kick that kid's ass if he so much as looks at you."

"Deal."

Chapter 10

We're just sitting down with our shakes at Fortinos when my phone alarm goes off. I check the display. "Shit."

Cameron takes a long pull on his shake and gives me a puzzled look.

"I'm supposed to be at the hospital in ten minutes. I have an appointment with Martinez." I throw my camera bag strap over my shoulder and lean over to give Cameron a kiss. "Sorry to cut this short."

"It's okay. I have this delicious shake to keep me company." He takes another sip. "Hey, if you love this place so much how come we've never come here before?"

I was hoping he wouldn't ask that. "I don't know. I

guess..." My mind scrambles for something that sounds plausible. "I come here sometimes with my mom after doctor's appointments."

He nods, his mouth never leaving the straw. For a moment I'm distracted by his lips and I'm tempted to skip the appointment for some quality time in Old Berta, but pissing off Martinez never ends well.

"Talk to you later."

I'm sweating when I burst into the waiting room of Martinez's office. "Sorry! My class ran late and then I forgot I had the appointment and was getting a shake with my boyfriend when my alarm went off and I got here as fast as I could."

The receptionist purses her lips. "He's running a few minutes behind. Take a seat." No 'please,' no 'don't worry dear.' Whatever happened to courteous receptionists?

I slump into a chair farthest from her ready to sulk until I'm called back, but I'm distracted by a mother quietly reading to her young son. Martinez is a brain doctor, which means either the mother or her son has something bad going on in their head. As far as the doctors are concerned, the mass they removed from my head wasn't cancer so I'm cured, or as cured as I'm going to be. They both have a full head of hair, which means neither of them have been at the mercy of his clippers. Suddenly my crappy day seems insignificant.

The boy twists around in his mom's lap to look at me. The lights in the waiting room are dim so I don't have to struggle to smile at him. He ducks his head against her arm, slowly peeking around the edge of her sleeve, and I laugh.

"Biz, it's nice to see you in a good mood." Martinez stands in the open door and I throw a scowl at the receptionist. "Come on back."

I wave at the little boy as I pass through the doorway.

I've lost track of how many times I've been in this office, but this is the first time I've been here with a migraine. I pull myself onto the examining table. Martinez is going to have a field day.

He wheels the padded stool closer to me and sits. "How are things going?"

I rub my hands on my knees. "Oh, you know. Some kid has decided I'm his latest entertainment, my boyfriend is being weird, but more of my pictures were published in the paper." How long can I keep him from figuring it out?

"I saw that. Congratulations. But you know I meant your head." He drums a pen on his knee. "When was your last migraine?"

Since I still have one, this isn't technically considered my last. "I'm not sure exactly. A couple weeks?"

He swivels to face the counter where my chart lies open. "Your mom hasn't refilled your prescription since before the surgery?"

"Sure." I don't know why he's asking me since it's all written in my file.

"Anything else I should know about? Light bothering you more than normal? Nausea?"

"Nothing unusual." All my symptoms are typical for when I flicker. Nothing new to report here.

"Okay, good." He swivels around to face me. "Up, please. You know the drill."

I slide off the table and stand in front of him, feet together. I close my eyes, ignoring the pulsing behind my eyes, and alternate touching hands to ears, raising my arms this way and that. I start to lift my leg and am falling before I realize it.

The stool clatters against the counter as Martinez jumps

to his feet. His strong hands catch me—one on my waist, the other cradling my neck—stopping me from cracking my head on the tile floor. The strength of his grip surprises me until I remember that he moonlights as an EMT. Those guys have to be able to lift 300-pound unconscious people; he could probably toss me over his shoulder with one hand. He lays me on the cold tile but doesn't move his hands.

I open my eyes and my breath catches in my throat. His dark brown eyes are inches from mine, searching my soul, trying to figure out what's going on inside my head. His fingers lightly squeeze the base of my neck.

"What happened there?" His voice is soft, throwing me back to the night we first met. Dad had been rushed to the ER and the ambulance lights made me have a fake-flicker—all the symptoms, none of the flickering—and Martinez just happened to be there when I stumbled. He stared into my eyes that night, too, but the concern on his face now feels more personal. He removes his hand from my waist and touches my temple, and I reflexively press my face to his hand.

He pulls back, putting a more professional distance between us, and I sit up, leaning against the side of the examining table and cross my arms tightly across my chest. I'm not quite sure what just happened, but the word 'inappropriate' flashes in neon in my head. "Sorry."

His eyes are still locked on mine. "Biz, talk to me."

"I lost my balance."

"Tell me or I'll drag you to get an MRI." No bluffing with him. He's throwing all his cards out on the first hand.

"You wouldn't."

His eyebrows raise and I swear I see a twinkle in his eye. "Try me."

I close my eyes and inhale slowly, hold it for a couple beats, then let it out just as slowly. "If I tell you, do you promise you won't make me get an MRI?"

"No."

I look at him. "That's not how this is supposed to work. I give a little, you give a little."

"This isn't a negotiation. We're talking about your health." He pulls away to lean against the counter behind him, taking his warmth with him. The cold from the tile seeps through my jeans. "I can't figure you out. I thought you'd want to know what's wrong with you, but you fight every test, every question. Some days I'm surprised you even show up to our appointments."

Me too.

"Are you going to level with me?"

His choice of words is ironic. What level of my malfunction am I willing to share? That I have a migraine? That I got it from flickering? That I flicker? His neurosurgeon brain would have an orgasm if he knew the shit going on inside my skull.

"Fine."

His eyes light up.

Cool it, buddy. I'm not giving you everything. "I have a migraine right now."

"Was that so hard?"

"Yes."

His mouth sets in a hard line. "Biz, I don't know what you think I'm doing here, but all I want is to help you. Do you want to have headaches the rest of your life?"

I immediately think of Dad. He doesn't get headaches anymore, but his symptoms are much, much worse. The prospect of ending up like him scares me more than I'd ever admit to Martinez. "They aren't so bad."

"I'd like to help you manage them and that starts with figuring out the trigger." He rubs his hand through his hair and I can't help noticing the similarity to Cameron. I wonder if Martinez has biceps that flex when he—I shake my head. Martinez sees the gesture and misunderstands its meaning. "You don't want to figure it out, or you don't want to tell me?"

I drop my gaze and he leans forward, elbows on knees, until his head is inches from mine.

"What aren't you telling me? Some days I wish I could look inside your head to see what's happening, but I've done that and I still don't know. I thought when we removed the mass the pressure on your temporal lobe would lessen and headaches would get better, but you're still suffering."

I peek at him without raising my head. He's having some kind of philosophical moment, staring over my shoulder. I exhale softly, relieved to have his focus off me, even if just for a moment. Telling him the truth would make things easier right now, but he's a doctor. He won't be satisfied with letting me flicker unless he understands the science behind it. True, I sometimes wonder what wires got crossed that make it happen, but not enough to spend the rest of my life being poked and prodded. No, thank you.

Martinez clears his throat, and our eyes lock again. Something in the soft brown depths tells me to trust him, to tell him my secrets, but I blink them away. I could get lost in there.

He reaches for my hand and cradles it between his. "Biz, you can trust me. I don't know what you're afraid of, but I'm not going to hurt you."

The heat from his hand feels safe, comforting. A small part of me wants to tell him. It would be so easy. Just spit it out and let the pieces fall where they may.

"Tell me the trigger."

The softness in his voice has taken on a sense of urgency and uneasiness twists my gut. I pull away. My voice cracks when I speak. "I can't."

Chapter 11

The rest of the week passes in a blur—more tests, more secretive texts from Cameron, and countless more encounters with Nate. Dad's waiting for me at the kitchen table when I get home, his folded hands resting on more brochures.

I sit at the chair across from him. "What's up?"

He pushes the brochures toward me and I spin them around. A different group of ethnically-diverse friends walks across a sunny green quad, ancient stone buildings resting stoically in the background.

"You really want to get rid of me, huh?" I meant it as a joke, but when I look up, Dad looks defeated.

"I want what's best for you. You don't feel it yet, but you'll want out of this town, to start new memories, and I don't want you to miss your opportunity because you're worried about me."

Panic grabs my heart. "Dad, what's going on? This isn't about colleges."

He studies the table between us for what feels like eternity before raising his head. When his eyes meet mine, my breath catches in my throat. "My latest test results haven't been good."

That's a fancy way to say the results are bad. He's been sick for so long that I was lulled into thinking he'd always be like this, that he'd never get worse. I wait for him to continue, but he remains silent. "What does that mean?"

He flattens his hands on the table. "My body is no longer reacting to the medication. The seizures are going to increase and eventually my nervous system is going to completely shut down." He sounds robotic, like he's reciting lines that someone else has written. "And now they say my liver and kidneys are failing."

My mouth goes dry. I can barely speak over the sudden lump in my throat. "How long—" I clear my throat. I can't believe I'm asking this. "Did they say how long you have?"

He turns away for a moment, and when he looks back at me there are tears in his eyes. "They wouldn't give me a specific time. I'm hoping I'll be able to see you graduate."

My breath stops. My heart stops. Dad cannot die. The lump in my throat climbs into my head and bursts out of me in a gush of tears.

He moves around the table to wrap me in his arms and I breathe in the clean scent of soap. His embrace is surprisingly strong, considering how weak he's become. "I knew this was coming. The doctors, they don't really know what's going on with me so I can't expect them to fix it."

I press my face so hard against his shoulder that the sharp angles of his bones dig into my cheek. All my life, my dad has been there for me. The one I turned to with skinned knees and failed tests and the occasional broken heart. Most of my friends were closer with their moms, but because of his illness, Dad's the one who was home, waiting for me after school with cookies and apple juice. I can't imagine coming home and not finding him here.

Another punch in the gut as I think of Mom. Her entire life revolves around taking care of him. Will I be able to fill that void for her?

He holds me close, not cluttering the moment with words that won't make a difference. Nothing he can say will change what he's already said: he's dying.

It wasn't long ago that we talked about the possibility of me dying, but even then, it didn't seem real. I was scared to double flicker since we weren't sure what would happen, but stopping the kidnapper was more important. This is different. There's nothing left to do.

"Is Martinez still pressuring you about your migraine triggers?"

I pull back so I can look him in the eye. "Yeah, why?"

"I'm wondering..." he pauses. "Maybe you should tell him."

"I don't know if it's safe." My appointment with Martinez earlier in the week plays through my mind. Sometimes his eagerness scares me.

He drops into the chair next to me, his hands covering mine. "Wouldn't you love to know why we flicker? Maybe we can prevent whatever's happening to me from happening to you."

I rub his sleeve between my thumb and forefinger. "Are

you sure we can trust him?"

"I would like to think so." He closes his eyes for a beat. "But I want to be there when you tell him."

"If you think I should, then I'll do it." I wipe my eyes, trying to push off the desperation I can hear in my voice.

He takes a deep, shuddering breath. Determination straightens his back and renews the light in his eyes. "He might be your only chance."

*****

Normally I sit on the couch with Dad and do homework until Mom comes home, but nothing about today is normal. Dad turns on a sitcom but I can't focus. His news has flipped everything all topsy-turvy. He's been sick my whole life and part of me has always known that maybe he wouldn't be around as long as my friends' dads, but hearing him say those words, that he's dying, feels surreal. And we're watching a show with canned laughter.

My phone beeps.

Amelia: You coming out?

Me: Not a good night.

Amelia: Come on! Trace's friends are
coming & I need my sidekick!

I smile.

Me: Since when am I the sidekick?

Amelia: Ha! See, you want to go.

Me: I don't know.

Dad looks up. "Is that Cam? We haven't seen him much lately."

Whatever lift Amelia brought to my mood vanishes. The corners of my mouth tug down. "Amelia wants me to go for pizza tonight but I told her I can't."

"It's Friday night. Of course you can."

I straighten against the back of the couch. My insides still feel raw, exposed. "How can you say that? How can I go out and pretend to act normal after what you just told me?"

"I don't want you to stop living your life just because I won't be here. The last thing I want is for you to spend all your time on this couch waiting for me to die."

His words strike me like a dagger to the chest and I burst into tears. "H–how can y–you say it like it's nothing?"

His face slackens, revealing all the years of pain and struggle that he's worked so hard to hide from me. And something else.

Relief? But how can he want to die? To leave me and Mom? He closes his eyes. "I'm tired, Biz."

I leap to my feet and am at his side in an instant. "Do you need help upstairs?"

He opens his eyes, his expression halfway between a smile and a frown. He reaches for my hand but doesn't move to get up. "I mean I'm tired of fighting. Of struggling to get through the day, just to wake up the next morning feeling the same. The doctors don't know what else to do for me and I'm okay with that."

I sink onto the couch next to him. He can't give up. Then a thought hits me. "What about Martinez? Maybe he can help you, too?"

He shakes his head. "My body is too worn out. Even if he was able to find a way to reverse the symptoms, I can't regenerate the parts of me that have stopped working."

That stops me. What if I've already done irreversible damage to myself? "But what about tests or research or something? If I really am just like you, don't you want to try to prevent the same thing from happening to me someday?"

"You're not going to let me give up, are you?"

"No."

"Let me think about it. I promise I'll go to an appointment with you, but I've been protecting my secret for so long..." He shakes his head. "I can't agree to tell someone that easily."

"Just promise you'll consider it, that's all I'm asking."

"Okay, I promise to consider it. On one condition."

"What's that?"

"You promise to stop flickering."

Chapter 12

I hide in my room until it's time to meet Amelia. Yes, I'm a coward. I know I should talk to Mom now that I know what's going on with Dad, but I've finally stopped crying and if I start again now I'll never leave the house. Besides that, I can't believe I promised Dad I wouldn't flicker anymore. It's one thing to decide for yourself that flickering to cheat isn't the best idea, but no one knew I'd decided to stop. Now I'll be letting Dad down if I don't keep my word.

I poke my head in the living room. "I'm meeting Amelia and some friends for pizza. I won't be too late."

"Nice to see you," Mom calls after me.

I ignore the little voice telling me I should stay home and

get into my car. I need a couple hours of pretending everything is okay. "Dad said he doesn't want me to stop living my life," I whisper to myself. I repeat it in my head until I arrive at our favorite pizza place.

Fricano's has been a staple in my town since I was a kid—really, since Dad was a kid—and as soon as the intoxicating smell of cheese and sauce and baking bread hits me the tension in my shoulders lessens.

Amelia waves from the huge booth in the far back corner and I head her way. Other kids from school are dotted around the restaurant, some with their families, others with friends, and I nod hello but don't stop to talk to anyone. I texted Cameron to invite him, but he wrote back that he's having family issues. What else is new? These days all he has are family issues.

I squeeze in next to Amelia. "Hey, everyone." Trace sits next to her. Heath and Aiden, two guys from the soccer team, flank a girl with long blond hair, who eyes me cautiously.

Trace gives a little wave. "Good, you're here. Maybe now Amelia will quit complaining that you never come out anymore."

Amelia elbows him in the ribs and he makes a little "what?"

face. "Everything okay at home?" she says low enough so no one else can hear.

I shake my head but don't say anything. Tears threaten to spill just thinking about Dad.

"Talk about it later?"

I nod, then clear my throat. "Did you order?" Glasses litter the table but it doesn't look like they've eaten yet.

Amelia snorts. "Yeah. Five pizzas."

The blond catches Amelia's eye and they giggle. "You'd think these guys haven't eaten in a week." Then the blond looks at me and the smile drops.

A twinge of jealousy bites me but I push it away. Amelia is allowed to have other friends. Like Trace said, I haven't been out much lately so of course she's going to hang out with other people. But why does it have to be scowly-McScowlerson?

"Do you know Christina?" Amelia asks.

"I've seen you in the halls. You're a sophomore, right?"

She lifts a shoulder as if to say whatever, then shifts her focus to Aiden.

I swallow back a smart-ass remark. I'm here for Amelia. I need to play nice. I give Amelia a nudge and whisper, "What's with her?"

Amelia glances at Christina but she's still staring at Aiden. "She's hot for that one and is just making sure you're not here to steal him."

I snort.

"I know, but give her a chance. She's cool when she's not being threatened."

"But I'm not—"

"You know what I mean."

I don't get to say more because our pizzas arrive—all five of them—along with two orders of breadsticks and two more pitchers of Coke. The boys reach for the pizzas, each claiming an entire pie and leaving two for the three of us girls.

"I don't know," I say. "This doesn't look like enough food."

Amelia laughs but the boys are oblivious. We each grab a slice and start to eat.

Christina twirls a strand of her long hair around a finger and gives me a curious look. "So what's with the hair? I know short is in but I could never cut mine off." She bats her eyes at Aiden but he's too fixated on his food to notice.

I reflexively touch the side of my head.

"Maybe if you put some product in it. Or wore a hat?" Christina gives me a nasty smile, one eyebrow raised in a gesture I'm sure she's practiced in front of a mirror, and I start to sweat.

Amelia ruffles the back of my head, careful not to mess up the top which I actually have styled to the best of my ability. When you've had long hair your entire life, short hair is like planting a new head on top of your shoulders. "I think it looks great. In fact, I was thinking of cutting mine, too."

Trace gives her a startled look. She squeezes his hand under the table as if to reassure him, but it makes me feel worse. I appreciate that she's trying to make me feel better but I know I look ridiculous.

Christina scoffs. "Whatever."

Trace rolls his eyes at her, then looks at me. "Cam couldn't come?"

I shake my head, grateful for the change in subject, even if it's another sensitive topic. "He stayed home. Family stuff."

Christina continues twirling her hair, her pizza untouched. "Isn't his sister the one who was kidnapped? What's her name? Katie?"

My blood boils at Katie's name on this girl's lips. I don't

care what Amelia thinks. This girl is a snooty bitch. "Yes."

She leans back, crossing her arms over her chest, and nods her chin across the room. "Isn't that her over there?"

We all turn and I spot Katie at a table in the opposite corner. She's with the girl that was with her at Fake Taco Bell, another boy I don't recognize, and Nate. If I didn't know better I'd say they were on a date. I turn back around and Christina is watching me, a triumphant smirk on her pouty lips.

"Guess he lied."

"Listen, you little—"

Amelia grabs my arm. "Biz, don't."

"No, this is bullshit. I came out to see you and Trace, not to deal with an insecure sophomore who needs to insult people to feel better about herself." I dig a ten dollar bill out of my purse and fling it onto the table. "I'm out of here."

Amelia follows me out of the booth and stops me at the next table. "I'm sorry. I should have known she'd be like that with you."

"What do you mean 'with me'?"

"You know, because you're so mysterious." She waves a hand up and down. "You aren't the most open person. People know you had brain surgery but no one knows why."

I tilt my head. "People think I'm mysterious? Is that a good or bad thing?" And why have I never heard this before? I knew I had a reputation for dropping guys after a month or two—well, before Cameron—but this is new.

A smile lifts one corner of Amelia's mouth and she glances back at our table. "Clearly some people think it's a bad thing. As for me, I just wish you'd trust me enough to tell me what's going on."

It's like she slapped me. I take a half-step back. "What do you mean? You're my best friend!"

She looks at her hands, which are twisted in the hem of her shirt. This has been on her mind for longer than just tonight. "Things haven't been the same for awhile. I know you're dating Cam—regardless of what Christina seems to think—but we're both supposed to be your best friend and it's like you don't trust me."

"Amelia, of course I trust you."

"Then why won't you tell me your big secret? I know you're keeping something from me."

My mouth opens but nothing comes out. After the day

I've had, it's taking all my energy to keep from curling up in a ball on the floor. I don't have it in me to convince Amelia how much she means to me.

"That's what I thought." Her words come out soft, unaccusing, but they sting far worse than anything Christina said.

"It's complicated."

"It wouldn't be a secret if it wasn't."

Touché. "I'm sorry. I wish I could tell you but I can't." My life would be so much easier if Amelia knew the truth, but the fear of being exposed keeps me from telling her.

"Then I guess you'll understand if I go back to the table."

I feel like she reached through my chest and ripped out my heart. Tears burn the back of my eyes. "Have fun."

I turn to walk away and my gaze falls on Katie. I need to find out if Cameron lied, but I'm not in the mood for more of Nate's charming personality. And since when do her parents let her out by herself? I take a deep breath and cross the room to their table. Cameron lying doesn't change the fact that I'm worried about her. I can't walk away without making sure she's okay.

"Hey, Katie."

She looks up and once again I'm startled by the change in her appearance. The black eyeliner is heavier than it was the last time I saw her and there's a fresh piercing in her eyebrow. "Hey."

"To what do we owe the honor, freak?"

I ignore Nate. I refuse to give him the satisfaction. "Cam said you guys were home tonight."

Nate leans into my field of vision. "Can't find your boyfriend?"

I scowl at him. "Shut. Up."

Katie shrugs. "He was home when I left."

"Okay, thanks." I pause, my gaze lingering on Nate. What on earth does she see in him? "Will you be going home soon? I could give you a ride."

Katie musses her hair so it falls in her eyes but doesn't answer me.

Nate's mouth twists into a sneer. "We don't want you here either."

I wait a beat longer, then adjust my bag on my shoulder and turn toward the exit. I hurry toward the parking lot, flinching at the insults Nate shouts after me and trying to ignore the creeping feeling that my day is only going to get worse.

Chapter 13

Driving to Cameron's, I can't stop worrying about Katie. Of all the people for her to hang out with, why does it have to be a complete jerk like Nate? Despite her tough-girl act, she's vulnerable and I'm afraid how much influence he has over her.

I've stopped myself from calling Cameron no less than ten times since I got in the car. He's probably just watching TV with his parents. Or in his room listening to music. I don't know what's going on and I've never not trusted him before, but the little voice in my head is telling me not to warn him that I'm coming over.

The lights are all on when I park in front of his house. I haven't been this nervous since our first date. I grip the steering wheel, then take a deep breath and climb out of the car. The doorbell is ringing before I can stop myself, and moments later I'm face to face with Cameron. My heart speeds up at the sight of him. His t-shirt is rumpled and his hair looks like he's been running his fingers through it for the past week. In other words, he looks amazing.

"Biz, hey. What are you doing here?"

I pause. You'd think I'd have figured out what I was going to say, but I was so anxious about what he was going to say that I didn't think this part through. "I was at Fricano's with Amelia and Trace and some of his friends and this one chick who is a complete B..." I realize I'm rambling and stop. I don't know how to say this without sounding like I'm accusing him of something. "Katie was there with that guy Nate, and you said you guys were staying home so I—"

"You saw Katie?" He looks over his shoulder toward the stairs. "But she's in her room. Are you sure it was her?"

Things start to click into place. I should have guessed that she snuck out. "Yeah. I talked to her."

He takes a step away from the door. "I should tell Mom."

I start to follow but something in his expression stops me

and I pause at the threshold. "Can I come in?"

His body stiffens but it's not his defensive stance. He looks awkward, uncomfortable. "I don't think that's a good idea."

That stupid lump lodges in my throat, but I refuse to cry.

His face softens. "I'm sorry. My parents..."

I won't break down in front of him, despite everything else that's happened today. "Whatever. I'll talk to you later."

He moves to close the door and something catches my eye down the hall. Or someone. I peek around his shoulder.

Sarah is standing in the hallway, a full glass of water in her hand.

Cameron follows my gaze, then turns back to me but his eyes don't leave the floor. "It's not what you think."

Anger pushes the sadness and hurt away and I need to move. I step through the threshold and try to push the door open further but Cameron grips my upper arms, stopping me from advancing.

"What is she doing here?" My voice comes out as a shout and I immediately wish I could take it back. I'm sure everyone inside heard me. I clear my throat and lower it a decibel. "You said you were having family issues. So now she's family?"

He moves me onto the porch and shuts the door behind us. "We need to talk."

I follow him, numb from what I just saw and scared shitless of whatever is going to follow that statement. Nothing good ever comes after "we need to talk." He opens Old Berta's passenger door and I climb in. Once he's seated next to me I look at him and wait.

And wait.

I don't want to be the one to start this conversation, but listening to nothing but our breathing is going to make me crazy. I reach out to touch his hand but stop when he looks at me. His face crumples. Is he going to cry? I don't think I can keep it together if he cries.

He pinches his bridge of his nose with his fingers and takes a deep breath. "Biz—"

"Don't say it," I interrupt. I don't want to hear this.

This time he reaches for my hand. I let him, savoring the warmth of his touch. "You know you're my best friend. But lately..." He shakes his head and my stomach plummets to my shoes. "I don't know. I adore you but—"

I wipe the corner of my eye. Don't cry don't cry don't cry.

"But now Sarah's in the picture."

"What? No. Biz, I don't know what I need to say to make you believe me."

"What else am I supposed to think? I really needed to talk to you earlier but you told me tonight was a family night. But then I saw Katie out with friends and Sarah's here." I glance at the house to see if Sarah's watching through a window, but I can't tell if anyone is there.

"She came over because she's having the same problems with her sister that I am."

"How convenient." I try to swallow the words but they're already out of my mouth and worming into Cameron's brain.

Any compassion that was on his face when we got in the car is now gone. "This is what I'm talking about. You don't like that I'm friends with Sarah but the fact that you can't seem to understand what our families are going through makes it impossible to talk to you. Katie and Maddy are both skipping class and ignoring anything our parents tell them, not to mention dressing like they're sixteen instead of twelve." He runs a hand over his face before looking at me again. "Biz, you aren't the only person with shit going on and I don't know what I need to say to make you get that."

The venom in his voice makes me flinch. We've fought before and I've heard him go off on other people, but I've never had so much of his anger directed at me. "I'm sorry. I don't mean to be insensitive, but sometimes crap spews out of my mouth before I can stop it. I know all this stuff with Katie has been hard on you."

"Do you?"

"Yes! Of course."

He turns away and stares at the steering wheel. "It doesn't feel like it."

"So what are you saying?"

He doesn't look at me. "I don't think I can do this right now."

Relief sweeps through me. He's right. We're both too emotional to talk about this right now. "Do you want to talk tomorrow? Maybe we can go for a drive or—"

"No. I can't do this." He gestures between us. "You and me."

My insides go numb. Tears slip down my cheeks and land on my hands, which are clutched in my lap. The silence hangs between us and I'm suddenly overwhelmed with an intense need to get away. I fumble with the door latch and open the door but before I can escape Cameron stops me with a hand on my arm.

"Biz, wait."

I face him, not caring that he sees me crying. "Why?"

"I don't want to leave it like this."

I smile bitterly and pull my arm away. "You can't have it both ways."

"I still care about you. I want to be your friend."

How many times have I said those words to a guy and never once meant it? "We both know how well that works out."

I open the door and climb out into the cool night air, leaving him sitting in the car, his hand resting in the space where I sat. I hurry to my car and manage to drive around the corner before I completely lose it. All I can think is I'm alone and he's back inside.

With her.

I park in front of a random house with lights blazing through the living room. A family I don't know sits in front of the TV and an aching sense of aloneness grips my heart and leaves me gasping for breath.

Everything is falling apart. I cheated to get on the front page. Amelia is so pissed off she's not speaking to me. Cameron is all but gone. And Dad—he might die before I can make things right and pull my life back together.

I lean my head against the steering wheel, tears falling onto my legs, unsure how I can go on.

Chapter 14

About the only thing I seem to have going for me right now is the fact that it's the weekend and I still have a week before the party. Between Dad's news, the fight with Amelia, and Cameron—my stomach clenches into a knot just thinking his name—I don't want to talk to anyone.

But I don't like laying here feeling sorry for myself. I need a plan, something to distract me from everything that's gone to crap around me. The college brochures are stacked precariously on the corner of my dresser. I'm still not convinced that leaving when Dad is so sick is the best idea, but since I apparently have no more friends maybe leaving wouldn't be so bad.

I crawl out from beneath the covers, toss the pile onto

the bed, and roll my shoulders. Time to get over this pity-party attitude. Amelia and I had a fight. She didn't end our friendship. As for Cameron... it's too soon to tell. I can't even begin to imagine my life without him, even if it is just as friends again, but I can't think about that right now. Time to focus on something else.

An hour later I'm covered in glossy brochures filled with pictures of smiling kids my age taking full advantage of their school's grassy fields. If you believed the brochures, all you do at college is play frisbee, lay on blankets, and maaaaaybe crack a book in between. Sure, there are well-lit shots of kids wearing safety goggles pouring colored water into beakers, but I won't be in those classes. I smile to myself. If I study photography I might be in one of the only classes that actually spends time outside.

Dad definitely did his homework when he picked which schools to look into. Most are within an hour or two from home, but a couple are on the northern west coast—Oregon and Washington—places where it rains more than it shines and, if I follow his thinking, there is minimal risk for flickering.

My heart swells. Even knowing that he's dying and probably

won't get to see me as an adult, he's still trying to give me the best that he can. I push the brochures aside and unfold myself from the blankets, then head downstairs.

"Well good morning, sunshine." Dad's at the kitchen table drinking coffee and reading the paper. He points at the stack of papers next to him. "No more pictures this week?"

I grab a cup of coffee and sit across from him. "No. I submitted a couple but my heart wasn't in it." But that's changing. From now on that's all I'm concentrating on. No friends, no boyfriends and their possible second girlfriends, no assholes at school who think I'm an easy form of entertainment. Combined with my promise of no more flickering, my transition to full-on loser will be complete in no time.

Dad smiles. "You're not bothered you didn't make the paper again?"

"I need to try harder. I've been distracted by other BS, but not anymore." I sip my coffee. "I was just looking through the brochures you gave me. You really put a lot of thought into these."

"I can't send my only daughter just anywhere."

"I tried to write my essay but you know me and writing..."

He looks down at his hands and flattens them against the table to stop them from trembling.

"Are you okay?"

He waves off my question. "It's a side effect of the latest medicine. What do you think of the schools in the Northwest?"

"They certainly have their benefits." I look over my shoulder toward the living room. "Is Mom here?"

He shakes his head. "Grocery shopping."

"It would be nice to not have to worry about accidentally flickering. But it's so far away." I pick at the corner of one of the newspapers. "I don't think I can leave you and Mom. Even a couple hours seems too far away and I can drive that. I'd have to fly any time something happened."

He closes the newspaper. "You wouldn't come home every time something happened."

"But—"

"Biz, at some point you need to start your own life and follow your dreams." He shakes his head. "That's what we want for you."

"I might consider it after..." Our eyes connect. "I can't believe we're talking about you dying like it's nothing. Dad, I'm not moving across the country while you're sick. Period."

"But you'll consider the closer schools?"

"Yeah."

"That's all I want."

I can't help but think he planned this all along. "You didn't really expect me to go so far away, did you?"

He smiles, and for a moment I can see the man from my childhood. "Does it matter?"

My eyes water and I have to take a deep breath to find my voice. "I love you, Dad. Thanks."

I spend the rest of the day alternating between homework and college entrance essays. I know the perfect story to wow the admissions people, but I'd rather keep my flickering a secret.

My phone's been silent all day. When the sky starts to darken I finally cave.

    Me: Hey.

Silence.

    Me: I'm sorry.

Silence.

    Me: Are you still mad at me?

Silence.

I'm about to toss my phone to the end of the bed when a series of texts come through.

Amelia: OMG hey!

Amelia: I'm sorry too! I miss you!

Amelia: I'm a little mad, but it's nothing a little secret revealing won't fix.

I laugh.

Me: Can we hang out tomorrow?

Amelia: Do you have something to tell me?

I pull my phone away and stare at it. Is she seriously blackmailing me?

Me: Serious?

Amelia: ;)

Amelia: Can you come over tomorrow?

Me: Sure. 1pm.

That gives me less than a day to decide if I should tell another person my secret.

Chapter 15

Hearing from Amelia gives me a burst of energy. I throw on last night's jeans and a sweatshirt, grab my camera bag, and head for the park. Yes, the park where Turner kidnapped me and where the events that led to Katie's recovery all started. I haven't been there since that day, but I've driven by and the light and shadows still call me. It's what first drew me to photography—the contrast of the shadows, finding a way to reveal what the light fails to capture—and I relish the similarities to my own life, the way light sends me hiding for the comfort of darkness.

I park at the far end and immediately regret coming. Cameron and I came here, too. My eyes fall on the spot where we accidentally put on a show for everyone in the park. I press my hands to my cheeks, trying to push down the heat, the tears, the stupid emotions that are turning me into a blubbering mess. The past is the past and while I can't change what's happened, it doesn't have to control me. Wiping my eyes with my sleeve, I hike my camera bag tighter onto my shoulder and head for the tree in center of the park.

Its mammoth branches spread in all directions, reaching through the blue sky to pull everyone beneath its protective cover. The sun is about an hour from setting and the shadows nearly touch the woods at the edge of the park. My heart stutters. That's where it happened, where Turner covered my mouth with a chloroform-soaked rag—so cliché I almost couldn't believe that's how he did it—and carried me to his van. I reflexively pull out my camera, but I don't want a picture. That memory is already burned into my head.

I turn my back on the woods to face the tree and feel nothing. Usually the moment my camera is in my hands a sense of calm focus puts me into a trance and I just react, but that's not happening today. I press the shutter anyway—click-click-click—capturing the branches where the leaves flutter in the breeze.

I wander the park for an hour, shooting without much thought, and leave dejected. This was supposed make me feel better. I know artists have off days but what if I can't produce when things aren't going well for me? Even worse, what if I only succeed when I flicker? Being at the right place at the right time is important, but I'll never make it as a photographer if I have to cheat to get the shot.

*****

Amelia's house is everything mine is not. Sunlight pours through oversized windows, curtains tied back to ensure no corner is left in shadow, and there's a freshness in the air that makes my house seem stale. Her room bears the closest resemblance to mine, despite her mother's best intentions. Clothes and shoes are everywhere, including on the bed, and gum wrappers litter the floor.

"Love what you've done with the place," I tease.

"My mom's threatening to ground me if I don't clean up, but who has time for that? We have a party to plan!"

I pause, nearly overwhelmed with everything that's happened with Dad and Cameron. "About that..."

"No way. Uh uh. You are having this party."

"But—"

"No buts. The entire soccer team is already planning to come."

"Oh yay, does that mean Christina will be there too? Maybe I can hook her up with Nate and they can make fun of me together."

"Probably. But it's not like you have to talk to her. Just tell Cam—"

She stops when I vigorously shake my head.

"What?"

I bite my lip to stop it from trembling. If I concentrate hard enough I can still feel the warmth of Cameron's hand, right before he ended things.

"Biz, tell me what's going on."

It comes out in a gush. "Friday after I left the pizza place I went to his house to find out why Katie was out when they were having family night and he was acting weird, then I saw Sarah inside and he wouldn't let me in and we broke up." All my strength leaves in that burst and I sink to the floor.

"What?! It has to be a mistake." She sits cross-legged in front of me. "Sarah was there?"

I nod.

She chews her lip and cracks her knuckles. I smile despite my grief. She means business. "So why did you break up?"

I study my fingernails. "Because I'm not being supportive enough. I 'don't understand what he's going through.'" I air quote the last part. "I'm trying, I really am, but of course I don't understand what he's going through. I care about Katie and want to help, but I don't know how. If he'd just talk to me instead of always turning to Sarah." The bitterness in my voice leaves a bad taste in my mouth. "Cameron seems to forget that I got kidnapped, too, just not for as long as Katie. Just because I got away—"

Amelia nearly falls over. "WHAT?"

Oh, crap. I look up, hoping my face doesn't betray my panic at my slip-up. "What?"

"You just said you got kidnapped."

Oh shit. Oh shit oh shit oh shit. I can't undo this.

She grabs my arms and brings her face so close to mine I can see flecks of light brown in her eyes. "What. Are. You. Talking. About."

Where do I begin?

Amelia sits back. "Is that your secret?"

If only that was it. My mind scrambles for a way that I can let her think that's all there is to it, but there would still be too many unanswered questions. Like how come no one knows I was kidnapped, since I flickered again and it technically never happened.

"Biz! Just tell me the truth. I'm your best friend and I don't know why you don't trust me, but I swear I would never tell anyone." She twists a strand of her hair, a less playful version of the earlier twirling. "I just want to know that you're okay."

My insides churn.

She stares at me, a combination of curiosity and concern playing on her features.

I can trust her, I know I can, but telling her goes against everything I've told myself since the first time I flickered.

She leans closer and grabs my hands. Her eyes search mine. "Are you dying?"

I shake my head, tears threatening to fall. It's not me who's dying.

"You're scaring me."

I wring my hands, unable to make the words come out. I'm

holding onto my secrets so tightly that I'm afraid once I start talking, I won't be able to stop.

Amelia watches me a beat longer before exhaling loudly and standing. She turns her back to me, arms crossed. "I thought I was your best friend but clearly that means nothing to you."

"Amelia, don't." I bite my lip. I can't lose her and Cameron in the same weekend. When I told Cameron I just spit it out because we needed to move quickly, but the words won't come. "It's hard to explain."

Her head turns slightly, listening.

"You know how I have a hard time with flickering lights?"

She snorts. "You could say that."

"It's not because it gives me migraines."

She spins around. "You've been faking your headaches?"

"No! God, no. I wish. But it's not the light that causes them."

"So what does the light do?"

I take a deep breath. "It makes me flicker—go back in time." I pause. "To the day before."

She slaps a hand on her dresser, as if to stop the room from spinning. "Stop the presses! Time travel is real!" Hey eyes roll so far back in her head that for a moment I wonder if she'll levitate.

"I'm serious."

"Time travel."

"Yes."

"As in, you leave this time and space and go someplace else."

"I don't leave this space, I'm always still here."

"So you can tell the future?"

I shake my head. "I only go backward. And it's only back one day. Well, a little less than a day. Although since the surgery it's been a full twenty-four hours." I still haven't figured out why that is.

She pauses to consider this. Several times she opens her mouth, but closes it without saying anything.

"It's the truth."

"Does Cam know?"

"Yeah."

The corners of her mouth droop.

"He hasn't known for long. I told him because I needed his help to rescue a little girl who'd been kidnapped. Cameron drove me to the boat ramp before dawn, and that's where I told him about flickering." I can still smell the humidity in the air as we raced away from the storm, trying to find sunlight so I could flicker. We had no idea Katie was still alive, but there were enough similarities between her case and the recent disappearances that I thought we might get some answers.

"I'm not following. What does—what did you call it? Flickering?—What does that have to do with a kidnapped girl?" She taps her finger on her lip. "Does this have anything to do with Katie?"

I nod.

"But the police found out it was Turner from an anonymous tip."

I point at my chest. "Anonymous. Well, technically my dad is anonymous. I was unconscious when he called."

She sinks to the floor in front of me. "Why wouldn't you want anyone to know you helped? Ohmigod, you could have had a parade in your honor."

I smile. "Yeah, that's exactly what I want. 'Hey everyone! Look at me, the freak!' No, thank you."

"I still don't understand what you did. You said you were kidnapped, too."

"It started with one of my photography assignments. I took pictures at the park of a little girl talking to a man near the woods, but didn't realize it until I downloaded the photos. Then that night on the news they reported that the same girl had disappeared. I sometimes flicker to help people—" I wink at her. "Trig tests, anyone?"

"That explains it! I could never figure out how you knew the answers!" Her smile lifts the weight in my chest and the anxiety I felt at telling her dissolves. I'm glad I can share this with her. Amelia had my back before she knew the truth, and it's comforting to know that her opinion of me hasn't changed now that I've unleashed flickering on her.

"Yeah. Robbie was right when he accused me of cheating, he just didn't have any proof."

She snorts.

"So anyway, when I heard about the little girl I knew I had a chance to save her. I had a picture of the man who took her. I knew exactly where to go." I shiver. "But when I went back to that day, everything was wrong. The girl was playing with her mom and the man—" I still have a hard time believing it was him. "—Turner, was there alone. He somehow knew that I'd figured out he was the kidnapper, and before I could get away, he drugged me and I woke up in a van."

Amelia's eyes widen.

"I managed to flicker out of the van and went back to the night before." I smile. "Totally freaked out Cameron. We were making out and I had blood all over my face."

She wrinkles her nose. "That sounds awesome."

"It really was. I told my dad what happened and he went to the police. Because I flickered back before I was kidnapped, it technically never happened."

"But it did."

"It did."

"So you saved Katie."

I nod.

"I guess I understand why you didn't tell me."

Relief sweeps through me. "I wanted to so many times. It would have been so much easier if you knew, but I was terrified of what would happen if my secret got out."

She's quiet for a moment. "That's a lot to take in." Her head tilts to the side. "Is the flickering why you had surgery?"

"Yeah. Flickering gives me migraines, but the double flicker that I did to get away from Turner put things over the top. When they cracked my head open they removed a mass and assumed that would help with the migraines, but nothing has really changed."

"So who knows the truth?"

"My dad and Cameron."

"Not the doctors? Not even Martinez?"

"No, but with everything that's happening with my dad I think I need to tell him."

She sits upright. "Hold on. What's new with your dad?"

I exhale and sink against the side of the bed. Tears pool in my eyes before I can speak.

Amelia is on her knees in a flash, grasping my hands. "Is it bad?"

"The doctors said he might not even make it to graduation."

Amelia falls forward to envelope me in a hug, a slower-motion version of her usual body tackle. "I'm so sorry. You should have told me last night."

I sniff and she pulls back. "I didn't want to bring everyone down. Especially with that ball-of-fun Christina."

"Yeah, she can be a bitch when she feels threatened. She likes Aiden and went into protective mode, but you're with Cam so it doesn't matter."

A fresh knife stabs me in the heart. "Was."

"Right. Sorry." She frowns. "I can't believe he's treating you like this after what you went through to save Katie."

"It's not that simple."

She bites her lip. "No, I suppose it's not."

I clear my throat. "So about the party..."

"Oh no you don't." Her shoulders straighten and she gets a determined look on her face. "You need this party more than ever."

Chapter 16

I spend the rest of the week doing my best to avoid Cameron but every time I turn a corner in the hallway I manage to run into him. If our school was bigger I could figure out a different route to my classes, but our lockers are in the same hall so I'm screwed.

Things get worse in photo class. I arrive late and the only open seat is directly across from him. He mercifully avoids eye contact, but I can't help but stare at his hands as they rest on the table. My heart aches at his nearness, and I want to tell him about my dad so badly that I nearly shout it for everyone to hear. I've never missed a guy like this and it's all I can do to keep it together. I'm out of my chair the moment Shelly excuses us. I want to give her more photos but I need to get away from him.

Friday arrives like every other day that week but with an added bonus: the party is tonight. Ameila's been delivering party supplies all week with the promise that she'll be over as soon as school lets out to help me decorate. Her idea of decorating means ten thousand neon paper pom-poms, a box full of battery-powered votive candles, and candy. Lots of candy.

Dad offered to help decorate, and even though he seems unchanged since getting the diagnosis, I told him we could handle it on our own. I'd feel terrible if he overdid it helping with a party that I don't even want to have. The only reason I haven't cancelled is I'm still hoping Katie shows up so I can try to talk to her. That, and I'm a little afraid of Amelia's reaction if I called it off.

I still haven't figured out how to handle the alcohol that I'm sure people are going to bring, but I'll deal with that when it happens. As long as people are chill and no one gets in a fight, my parents shouldn't notice from upstairs.

The doorbell rings shortly after I get home and Amelia bursts through the door, plastic bags hanging off each arm and a hot pink feather boa wrapped around her neck. She peeks into the living room, then glances at the stairs. "How's your dad?"

I shrug. "The same. The only thing that's different is we know—" I cut myself off. "He offered to help but I assumed you have things under control."

She smiles. "You assumed correctly." She unloads the bags on the kitchen island and pulls her MP3 out of her back pocket. "I figured you didn't make a playlist." She walks to the living room and kneels in front of my parents' stereo. "Does this have a USB port?"

"Bottom left corner."

She pulls a cable out of her other pocket and moments later music blares from the speakers. "Light 'em up-up-up, light 'em up-up-up, light 'em up-up-up, I'm on FI-RE!"

I raise an eyebrow. "Probably not the best song to start off. Don't want my parents camping down here the entire time."

Amelia presses the volume button and the wailing softens. She stands and gives me a wry smile. "Perfect. Now let's get decorating."

"Is it too late to cancel?"

"Yep."

"How many people do you think will come?" In the movies the house is empty and the host thinks no one is coming, then the doorbell rings and the entire school is standing on the front lawn. I can't decide if that would be the best or worst thing to happen. If no one shows, I'm a loser, but if everyone comes it'll be so crowded I can sneak away and hide in my room.

Amelia tilts her head, thinking. "Two hundred?"

My mouth drops. "What? There's no way my—"

She laughs. "I'm kidding. Calm yourself. I'd guess thirty, but who knows. High schoolers can be fickle." She paws through the bags on the island. "Now where's that disco ball?"

I throw a pom-pom at her head. Maybe this won't be so bad.

Five hours later the ceiling is covered with neon paper balls, softly lit by the candles. A mix of bluegrass rock plays at a talkable level. Bowls of candy are strategically placed where we guessed people will congregate and the fridge is stocked with every flavor of soda known to man. My parents refused my suggestion to enjoy a night on the town, but are camped out in their room with the promise to stay there unless something breaks or they hear a chainsaw. They must be thinking of the same 80's movies I am.

Amelia and I are flopped on the couch, catching our breath before people arrive, but a flutter of excitement keeps me from sitting still. I wander the living room, adjusting candles and pressing the tape holding the pom-poms in place.

"Thanks for doing this. I know I haven't been the most cooperative—"

"You? Noooo..."

"Shut it."

"You're welcome." Amelia leans forward on the couch, elbows resting on her knees. "This will be fun."

Nerves shoot from my head through my toes. I point at her as the doorbell rings. "It better be."

Trace saunters into the kitchen, followed by Aiden, Heath, and another guy from the soccer team that I've never met. I peek around the corner. No Christina, thank god.

Amelia rushes to Trace's side and gives him a quick kiss. "Hey, thanks for coming early."

I stare at her in awe. She put more planning into this than I realized. I need to stop being such a baby. I move to the fridge and yank open the door. "Help yourself to soda. There's candy and chips and stuff all over the place."

Trace reaches past me and grabs four cans, setting them on the island. Aiden and Heath continue a conversation from before they arrived and just as I lean on the counter the doorbell rings again.

By ten o'clock the party is most definitely a success. A handful of kids from my photography class are camped out on the sofa, giving them prime viewing for the pseudo-dancing going on in the middle of the living room, and Amelia has a group of people cracking up in the kitchen. Candy-fueled energy keeps people from sitting still for too long, but I can't help but watch the door for the one person I know isn't coming.

I touch my hair for the millionth time. Amelia convinced me to try a new product that coaxes the curls into something resembling a style, but I miss the security of my knit hat. I stroll as casually as I can toward the bathroom to check the mirror, but there's already three people waiting in line. Turning back toward the living room, I hear the door open and my heart does a little flip, but it crashes the moment I see who it is.

Christina.

And she brought two equally cheerful friends.

This may be my party but I'm not talking to her. Fortunately she spots Aiden in the kitchen and beelines for his side. Her friends wander around the island, finally settling near her elbow, just outside the group.

So she's the leader.

I join my classmates on the couch, hoping the conversation about a famous National Geographic photographer will distract me, but I've barely figured out who they're talking about when the door opens again and my night gets worse.

Chapter 17

Katie walks through the front door, followed by Sarah's sister Maddy, Nate, and another guy. Katie seems unsteady on her feet, but it could be the platform heels strapped to them. I fight the protective instinct that urges me to help her and stay seated on the armrest.

Several heads turns as they make their way through the kitchen, but no one seems as floored by her appearance as I am. Most people have only seen her picture on the news where she looks like a normal twelve-year-old, not this creature who could pass for several years older. They probably don't realize who she is.

Nate stops at the fridge and looks inside. He says something over his shoulder to Katie, who shrugs, then takes a can of cola from him. He sets three more on the counter, then pops them each open and pours some out of each can into the sink. He pulls something from the inside pocket of his jacket and while I can't see what it is, it's obvious he's pouring something into the cans. They each grab a can, do a half-hearted toast, then continue into the living room.

I straighten, readying myself for whatever verbal attack Nate has planned, but he ignores me. Katie catches my eye for a second, a tense moment that I can't decipher—Is she asking for help? Telling me to stay away? Daring me to confront her?—then huddles closer to Nate. I don't believe this will be so easy, and I can't allow myself to relax. Things have gone smoothly so far and my gut tells me that something's going to happen. I want to move closer to Amelia but I don't dare draw attention to myself.

My phone buzzes.

Amelia: Should you tell Cam she's here?

Me: I'll keep an eye on her.

Amelia: Okay. Me too.

A loud squeal followed by a crash has me running to the kitchen. Christina stands over a pool of soda, an amused smile on her face. She tilts her head but makes no move to clean it up. "My bad."

I grab a bunch of paper towels and throw them onto the floor.

Christina turns back to the group but her feet are still in the puddle.

My fists clench. I really really want to shove her out of the way. Instead I clear my throat. "Can you move?"

She tosses her hair over her shoulder and purses her lips. "Oh, am I in your way?"

I cock my hip and nod at the mess. "I thought you'd notice that you pissed yourself, but I guess not."

Everyone at the island laughs and her smile disappears. She leans closer. "You know that's soda."

"Do I? I was in the other room."

She points at the can on the floor but I stop her before she speaks. "Get out of my way."

She huffs out a breath and rolls her eyes. "Whatever." She moves to the other side of Aiden, leaving me to kneel on the floor to clean up her mess.

Nate chooses that moment to attack. "Looks like you found your calling, freak."

I don't look up, but anger burns in my chest. "Why are you even here?" And what does Katie possibly see in him?

"I was invited. Heard there'd be a freak show." He laughs and my skin crawls. I can feel his eyes burning into the back of my head. "Although I thought it'd be a little more entertaining than this."

"Don't you have a puppy to kick or something?" Amelia's voice cuts through his laughter.

I turn toward her voice just as Nate cocks his leg like he's going to kick me, and I throw my hands in front of my face.

"Hey!"

"What the hell!"

Chairs scrape against the linoleum and I'm surrounded by bodies. I hear a loud thump and a heavy exhale and risk looking up. Trace and Heath have Nate pressed against the refrigerator. Heath's arm is wedged against Nate's windpipe, and Nate doesn't even struggle. He's no match for the stars of the soccer team. They may not use their arms in the games but they are pure muscle.

Amelia's at my side, pulling me to my feet. "When did this start?"

"I don't know. A couple weeks ago." I'm still holding the wet paper towels, and for a moment I forget how they got there. "He doesn't like my hair."

"What is wrong with people? I was joking about the puppy, but seriously, doesn't he have something else to do with his time?"

Heath loosens his grip on Nate so he can speak.

"I wasn't going to hurt her. I was just messing around."

Trace shoves him and he stumbles. "It's time for you to leave."

I glance toward the stairs. My parents have to be hearing this. The last thing I need is my dad worrying about me, not to mention trying to break up a fight. I touch Trace's arm. "It's okay. Just forget it."

Trace turns to look at me and Nate charges at him, knocking him into the island. Chairs go flying, crashing into the wall. Trace catches himself on the edge of the island and ducks Nate's fist, grabbing Nate and using his momentum to toss him into the living room.

Nate lays stunned for a moment, then scrambles to his feet, straightening his shirt. His entire body is tense, a slight tremor running from his shoulders to his fists.

Katie wobbles to his side from the corner of the living room. She reaches for his arm but he doesn't notice her.

I step toward Katie and try to pull her away from Nate. "He's a jerk. Why are you with him?"

Her eyes focus on mine and she frowns, a sad expression that goes beyond her concern for Nate, and for a second I think I've finally reached the girl hidden beneath this tough girl facade, but then she turns away, her lips tight. "You wouldn't understand."

Trace moves so he and Nate are toe-to-toe, Heath at his side. "Time to go."

You wouldn't think the sound of a door opening on a different floor would have any effect on what's happening on the main floor, but everyone freezes. Mom walks calmly down the stairs, runs her eyes over every single person in the room, then heads for the fridge. She grabs a couple sodas, then faces us. "Everyone having a good time?"

Her voice is friendly but her eyes are hard as she scans each face, searching for the troublemakers. She lingers on Nate and Trace, then walks over to me and plants a kiss on my cheek.

"Not too loud, okay?"

"Okay, Mom."

The room exhales as she climbs the stairs. Nate slinks away from Trace and Heath and tugs Katie into the corner of the living room. He pulls her against him and my stomach clenches as she leans willingly into his arms. She's too young to be acting this way. I need to put a stop to this.

I take a step toward her, when Trace rests a hand on my arm. "You okay?"

"What?" My mind is on Katie and it takes me a second to figure out what he means. "Yeah. He didn't actually touch me." A sense of deja-vu hits me. I said those same words to Cameron just a few days ago. The warmth of Trace's hand brings tears to my eyes. Cameron has always been the one protecting me. Without fail, if I needed help, he was there. But not tonight. "Thank you for looking out for me."

He smiles. "What are friends for?"

The pain in my heart lessens a little. All this time I hadn't thought of Trace as a friend, just as Amelia's boyfriend, but I guess he is. Maybe I haven't given him enough credit.

Amelia rushes up and wraps her arms around him, nearly

knocking him off his feet. "My hero!"

I laugh, grateful for Amelia being Amelia. The tension in the room fades and people go back to whatever they were doing before Nate busted into the room. Speaking of... he's not in the living room anymore.

And neither is Katie.

There's nothing you can do, I tell myself. But there is. She's just a kid and she's been through so much and even though Cameron isn't talking to me right now, I still love Katie like a sister. My bond with her started long before I had romantic feelings for Cameron. I can't just stand by and watch something bad happen to her. I need to be the big sister I keep claiming to be and help her.

I step further into the living room, hoping they're hiding in a corner and I didn't see them. Nope. Trace told him to leave but I didn't see them go out the front door. Where else could they be?

My stomach turns as my gaze falls on the stairs. Please don't let them be in my room. I head for the stairs just as a scream pierces the air. Followed by another scream.

A door opens and Nate runs down the stairs. Without

looking at anyone, he rushes out the front door, closing it firmly behind him. Heath and Trace exchange glances.

"Go!" Amelia shouts, and the two rush after Nate.

I take the stairs two at a time and bust into my bedroom, but there's no one there. Where is Katie?

Dad appears in the hallway. "Do we need to step in?"

"I don't know. I don't know where she is."

He nods at the closed bathroom door. "It came from there."

I reach for the knob, but hesitate. I knock instead. "Katie, are you in there?" I press my ear to the edge of the door. "Katie, it's Biz. Can I come in?"

A drawer opens and closes, then another. Dad touches my shoulder. "Go in. We'll be right here if you need us."

"Okay." I turn the knob, not expecting it to open, but it does. Katie is squatting in front of the vanity, rummaging through the bottom drawer. I close the door behind me. "What are you looking for?"

She slams the drawer shut and slumps over so she's sitting next to the toilet, avoiding my gaze. "Nothing." The little girl I once knew is gone. I couldn't see it before, but here on the bathmat, with her torn tights and disheveled top, I realize I don't know this person.

I lower to the ground so I'm at her level. My gut tells me that whatever she was looking for, it can't be good. Aside from migraine medicine, the only dangerous thing in here are razors, but those are in another drawer. The desperation on her face scares me. I lean against the vanity so she can't get into that one. "Did Nate hurt you?"

Her lip curls in a sneer, further transforming her into someone different. "Hurt me? No."

"I heard you scream."

She shrugs.

I risk touching her arm, barely feeling the fabric of her top, and she flinches.

"Katie, what's going on? I'm worried about you."

Her back straightens and she glares at me, the desperation replaced with anger. "Not you, too. It's bad enough my family's all over my case, constantly checking on me to 'see how I'm doing'." She air quotes the last part. "How do you think I'm doing?"

"Horribly." It's out of my mouth before I can stop it.

Her jaw drops, but she doesn't contradict me. She pulls herself to her feet and paces the room, three steps back and forth, bumping into me. I stand and press my back to the door to give her space. She's even more unsteady than she was earlier.

"How much have you had to drink?"

She whirls on me. "What difference does it make?"

I grip the edge of the counter. This is new territory for me and I don't want to screw it up. If she won't talk to her parents or Cameron, maybe she'll trust me.

"Save it. I don't want to hear it."

My breath comes quick and I inhale deeply to clear my head. "I can't begin to understand what you're going through, but I do care about you. You've been like my sister for as long as I can remember and while I may not be a part of your family—" my heart aches thinking about how far from her family I am now "—you're still important to me."

She stops pacing and leans her backside against the opposite end of the counter from where I'm standing. "I want to go home."

Last I saw Nate he was running out the front door, but I wouldn't let her leave with him anyway. I force out the words I don't want to say. "Do you want me to call Cam?"

"I thought you broke up."

"He's still your brother. And I care about you."

She's quiet for several minutes, but I wait her out. "Fine. Whatever."

I pull my phone from my back pocket and text him before she changes her mind.

> Me: You need to come get Katie from my house.

"Where's Nate?"

"He left. We heard you scream so some of the guys followed him." I leave what they probably did to him unsaid.

A sob bursts from her throat. "But it's not his fault!"

I don't try to hide the confusion on my face. "Katie, I'm sorry to keep asking, but what the hell happened?"

Her shoulders shake and she covers her face with her hands.

I rest my hand on her shoulder. "Katie—"

"Don't touch me!" She jerks away, pressing against the wall near the tub. Mascara is smeared around her bloodshot eyes, her cheeks wet with tears. "That's the problem. I can't do this."

I'm almost afraid to ask. "Do what?"

"Be normal around boys."

"Katie, no one expects you to—"

"I'm never going to be better. Not after what that bastard did. I'm ruined and now Nate knows it too."

154

I reel back. I already know the details, that Katie was raped countless times over the four years she was gone, but hearing her say it knocks me off balance.

"I invited Nate in here." She looks me in the eye, surprisingly steady for how wobbly she was a minute ago. "But I'm never going to be able to be go out with a guy."

My phone dings.

Cameron: On my way.

She folds her arms over her chest. "Is that Cam?"

I nod.

"Great."

"Can I help you clean up?" I gesture at her face.

"What's the point? There's no cleaning me up." She crosses the bathroom and flings the door open. She's down the stairs before I can stop her. There's an audible gasp as she moves through the kitchen and I rush after her. The front door is open so I step outside. She's sitting in a pool of light on the front step, shoes on the ground next to her, head in her hands.

I sit next to her, steeling myself to see Cameron.

Chapter 18

Katie has stopped crying by the time Old Berta comes to a stop in the middle of the street. Cars fill the driveway and the edge of the grass on the side of the road so there's no place else for Cameron to park. Katie stands but I can't move. The cold concrete chills me to my core and I can't trust myself not to run to him and fling myself into his arms. So I sit.

Berta's door creaks open and I hold my breath. Don't cry. Don't freak out. And certainly don't wrap myself around his feet and beg him to take me back.

Cameron half-runs through the front yard and jerks to a stop when he sees us. His eyes widen as he takes in Katie's appearance, and in seconds he's at her side, gripping her arms.

"Are you okay? What happened?"

She shrugs. "Not my best night. Can we go home?"

He glances at me then back to her. "Yeah. Get in the car. I need to talk to Biz for a second."

She grabs her shoes, then steps past him without a word. I feel like I'm watching her inch closer to her self-destruction, her body crumbling as her mental suffering threatens to overwhelm her entire being.

"Good night, Katie."

She looks over her shoulder. "Thanks, Biz." She walks better without the shoes and I have to wonder if she isn't as drunk as I suspected. But that thought evaporates when Katie gets into the backseat of the car. Someone's already in the front.

For a second I'm worried I might actually throw up. I can't look at him. What if he was telling the truth about Sarah and I've pushed them together? Maybe Cameron's right. I haven't been a very good girlfriend. But then again, he tells me so little that it's sometimes hard to know what he wants from me. From the corner of my eye I see him watching me, and I meet his gaze.

He moves toward the step like he's going to sit next to me, then changes his mind. "Thanks for looking out for her."

I nod.

"What happened?"

How much should I tell him? If this is Katie's normal behavior then this shouldn't be news to him, but I don't want to repeat what Katie said about Turner. "She showed up drunk but was pretty quiet until just before I texted you. That's when she started screaming."

He inhales sharply.

"Nate came flying down the stairs and I found her in the bathroom."

His body goes rigid. "Nate?"

"The one and only. Trace and his friends took off after him and I can only imagine how that went."

"Good. He better make himself invisible or I'll kill him."

I study my fingernails before continuing. "Is she getting help? Talking to someone?"

He nods slowly before sitting next to me. Not so close that we have any chance of accidentally touching, but closer than he's been in a week.

I close my eyes and try to imagine the heat from his body comforting me after all the crap that happened tonight.

"She stopped going."

My eyes snap open and I look at him. "Cam, she's got some serious problems."

"I know."

"Do you?" I picture her digging through the drawer in the bathroom. How much has Katie shared with him?

"You're not telling me everything that happened."

I stretch my arms in front of me, stalling. Telling him what I saw will only hurt him more, and while he needs to know what happened, maybe I can gloss over the details. "I know you're doing your best to help her, but you need to try harder. Make her go back to the doctor." The desperation in Katie's eyes scared me but I don't know how to tell Cameron what I'm thinking. "Don't let her push you away."

"My mom's been trying. The hearing is coming up and Katie's been even more distant than usual."

The hearing. I knew it was coming but I've only thought about it as a distant, far-off thing, not an event that's quickly approaching and threatens to tear his family apart all over again. Katie's behavior makes a little more sense now. If I were her I'd be freaking out, too. "Don't give up on her, Cam."

He's quiet for several minutes, so long that I wonder if he heard me, his body still. "I miss you. This is the longest we've ever gone without talking."

I miss him, too. So much it's a physical ache in my chest. There are moments I fear it will completely overwhelm me. I look at his car. "Is that Sarah in the front seat?"

He follows my gaze and his face falls. "Yeah."

His miserable expression is the only thing that keeps me from disintegrating. If he was with her he'd be happy, right? Or if not happy, given the situation with Katie, not so defeated. This small glimmer of hope gives me the courage to say what I do next. "So is this over?"

His eyes meet mine and I instinctively lean closer. But he stays where he is. "I don't want it to be."

I can feel the tears coming, a ball of pressure creeping up my throat that stops my breathing.

"I've been thinking a lot. I care about you, that hasn't changed, but I need some time."

The ball hardens. I take a deep breath, forcing it back into my belly where I can deal with it. "I'm not going anywhere. If you need me, even if it's just to talk, I'm here."

In a quick movement he reaches over and squeezes my hand, then releases it and gets to his feet. "Thank you."

I flex my fingers. They're cold from the night air except where he touched me and I swear if I look hard enough I can see marks where he warmed my skin.

"I've gotta go. Thanks for helping her."

"Uh-huh."

He gives me one last look before walking slowly to his car. To Sarah. When he opens the door the overhead light comes on and I see her for a moment, but then he slams the door and they fall into darkness.

The neighborhood is quiet for a Friday night. Grown-ups who've gone out to dinner are probably all home, and the kids my age haven't come home yet. I haven't looked at a clock in a while but my guess is it's close to midnight, so people will need to leave soon. I smile to myself. Even Amelia can't argue with that.

As much as I'd rather stay on the front step the rest of the night, I drag myself back inside. Trace and Heath are at the island, hands waving as they recount what they did to Nate. Christina's blond friend is glued to Heath, eyes wide, but Christina isn't in the room. I try to catch Amelia's eye but she's as entranced as the rest of the group. Whatever, I'll worry about Christina when I see her.

Cups litter the living room floor, leaving a kaleidoscope of soda on the carpet. I sigh, feeling even more beat down than before. I gather the cups off the floor then move around the group in the kitchen to throw them away.

Heath has everyone's attention. "After Trace tackled him into the neighbor's front yard, Nate started blubbering like a little baby. 'I didn't do anything. Please stop.' Fricking douche. No one makes a girl scream like that for not doing anything."

The blond fawns. "You're a hero!"

My stomach turns. Nate was telling the truth, and aside from Katie I'm the only one who knows, but after the way he's tormented me the past couple weeks I can't bring myself to defend him. I pause by Amelia and lean close to her ear so the others can't hear. "It's almost midnight."

She winks. "About to turn into a pumpkin?" She's been drinking, too, but just enough to make her silly.

I roll my eyes. "More like my parents are about to turn into wicked stepmothers. Will you help me get people to leave?"

She sighs dramatically. "Fine. I don't need to hear this story a fifth time anyway."

"I'm going to make sure no one's upstairs." My crowd of friends aren't the type to sneak into a bedroom when the parents are home, but these are Trace's friends. My bedroom door is closed, as I left it, and no light shines from beneath the door. I press my ear to the door and listen. It's quiet for a moment, but then I hear a muffled giggle. Great. I knock lightly, not wanting my parents to overhear, and the giggles grow louder, followed by low voices. I wait a moment but no one comes to the door, so I take a deep breath and turn the knob.

Light from the hallway spills onto my bed, onto Christina, who's lying half naked on my sheets with Aiden kneeling over her. A flimsy bra barely contains her breasts, and from the placement of Aiden's hands, if I'd showed up a few minutes later that bra would be on the floor with the rest of her clothes.

"Get the hell out of my bed," I whisper in as threatening a tone as I can manage. If I could direct the anger I'm feeling into my voice it would shoot lasers through his perfectly toned abs.

Aiden turns his head, acknowledging me, but Christina's focus remains on his bare chest.

"Now."

I close the door so they can get dressed.

Minutes tick by and they still haven't appeared.

I open the door again but close my eyes. "Now!" I hear a zipper, followed by more giggling, and risk a look.

Aiden is pulling his shirt over his head while Christina prances around my room in her bra and underwear.

"Are you stupid? Get dressed and get out of my house."

Aiden hands Christina her clothes and she finally looks at me, barely restrained challenge in her eyes. "You might want to wash your sheets."

This time I slam the door and take the stairs two at a time. The living room is cleared out but most of Trace's group is still gathered around the island. Amelia raises an eyebrow at me, but before I can respond I hear footsteps on the stairs.

"Time to go home, everyone." Dad's voice is calm, relaxed. If he heard me upstairs, he's not letting on.

Amelia rushes over and gives him a hug. "Thanks, Mr. Biz. We were just about to leave."

Within five minutes Dad and I are alone, surrounded by a sea of plastic cups and chip and candy wrappers. "You know

164

where the trash bags are," Dad says with a smile. "At least they didn't break anything."

Maybe he won't notice the carpet until the morning. I'm opening a trash bag when the stairs creak. We both turn to see Christina and Aiden tip-toeing into the kitchen.

Dad crosses his arms and looks down his nose at them. It's the most intimidating I've seen him in years. "I'm sure your parents are wondering where you are."

A blush creeps up Christina's face and for once she keeps her mouth shut.

"Sorry, sir," Aiden mumbles as they rush to the front door.

Dad swivels to face me, arms still crossed.

"I tried to get them to leave."

"Is that what was going on here?"

"No! I mean, I guess they were, but I don't even like her. I sure as hell didn't give her permission to go in my room."

"If you don't like her, why was she here?"

"Another chance to make my life miserable? Who knows."

I sweep my arm across the island, dumping cups and trash into the bag in one movement. "Do we really need to do this right now?"

He takes a deep breath and rubs a hand over his chin. "It's not like you to let people treat you badly. I seem to recall you getting suspended when a boy accused you of cheating."

I smirk. "But I was cheating." Only Dad knows the truth about that.

"True enough. What's going on that you're letting people you don't like into our home?"

I wave an arm in frustration. "Have you seen me lately? I look like a freak!" But he makes a good point. Normal people don't let total bitches into their house, and if they do, they sure as hell don't let themselves get walked all over in front of their friends.

"You had brain surgery. Your hair was a small sacrifice to—"

"Tell that to the kids at school." I continue cleaning, but silently I vow to be better about standing up to the Nates and Christinas of the world. It's not like it can get worse. "Can we do this later? I'd really like to go to bed." My bed that Christina just did god-knows-what in. I shudder.

"One last thing. Is Katie okay?"

I drop the bag and slump onto the island, my forehead landing in something sticky. "No, she's not okay. She's a mess and I don't know what to do to help her."

"I'm sure her family is doing everything they can. What does Cam say?"

I clench my eyes, grateful Dad can't see my face. "Cam and I haven't exactly been talking lately."

He's quiet for a moment, then exhales softly. "Oh."

I straighten. "Yeah." I look around the room. "Can I finish this in the morning?"

The stern look is gone. "Wipe off the counter and you're good."

"Thanks, Dad." I move around the island and kiss his cheek. "Good night."

Moments later I'm standing in my doorway, glaring at my bed. I cannot believe that skank was in here. Without turning on the light I grab a corner of the sheets and yank all the bedding so it's folded over, then toss it across the room. There's a fleece blanket on the desk chair that will have to do. I wrap it around my shoulders then flop face-down onto the mattress, but the mix of anger and frustration and sadness coursing through me won't let me sleep. I can't let tonight end this way.

As soon as I'm done cleaning in the morning, I'm flickering. I know I said I'd stop, but this isn't for me. This is for Katie.

Chapter 19

Mom's in the kitchen drinking coffee when I come downstairs.

"Morning."

She raises an eyebrow and gives me a once over. "Still wearing last night's clothes? Good party, huh?"

"You didn't talk to Dad?"

"He said he came down around midnight to send everyone home and they did." She sips her coffee, watching me over the brim. "I did hear Katie, but other than that, did anything happen I should know about?"

I slide into the seat next to her, suddenly realizing that the mess I'd left here is gone. No more cups. No more stickiness.

Even the stuffed garbage bag is no longer in here. "Did you clean?"

"Me? No. I figured you did before you went to bed."

I swivel around to look in the living room. Except for the stains on the carpet, all evidence of the party is gone. "Dad shouldn't have done that." One more reason to go back. Dad shouldn't be cleaning up after me—I should be helping him.

She follows my gaze. "Looks like he left you the floors. I'll give you money to go rent one of those cleaners from the store."

I'll be sure to flicker before then.

*****

After breakfast I'm heading to the store when my car practically drives itself to the Strand. I make a mental note to keep an eye on the people in the living room to stop them from spilling on the floor and to clean throughout the party so Dad doesn't try to help.

My breathing slows as the trees approach. To think I was worried that I'd lost this, just when I was starting to realize how to use my ability to help other people. Katie needs me. I don't know if stopping Nate will make a difference, but it's all I have right now.

Flickering light fills the car, a series of strobing flashes that I used to dread, but now long for like a drug. My fingers start to tingle and I press the accelerator. The tingling spreads to my toes, then the crushing weight pushes me lower and lower into the seat. Careful to keep the car moving in a straight line, I hang on until the weight lifts and I'm rising up, up—

—and I'm sitting on the toilet at school. Of all the situations to flicker back to, this is my favorite. It's always a little weird to suddenly find your pants around your ankles, but there's no one around to witness my spastic reentry.

I check the time on my phone and do a quick calculation. Privacy has its perks but at least when I flicker into class I don't have to figure out which class I'm supposed to be in. I hustle down the hall, already plotting how to help Katie. If I manage to fix the party in the process, even better.

*****

"Thanks for doing this. I know I haven't been the most cooperative—"

"You? Noooo..." Amelia says.

"Shut it." I sometimes wonder how I remember exactly what

I said the first time, but I just open my mouth and it comes out.

"You're welcome." Amelia leans forward on the couch, her elbows resting on her knees. "This will be fun."

I point at her as the doorbell rings. Nervous energy still runs through me, but since I already know the worst that will happen, I'm actually a little excited. "It better be."

Trace saunters into the kitchen, followed by Aiden, Heath, and the other guy from the soccer team. Still no Christina.

Let the fun begin.

I wander between the kitchen and the living room, too anxious for things to happen to settle down.

"You're making me crazy." Amelia tilts her head to one side. "You know something I don't?"

This is the first time I've flickered since telling Amelia my secret. I'm not sure how she'll react if I tell her, but it might distract me from waiting for Christina, Nate, and the rest of the let's-make-Biz's-life-a-nightmare crew. I lean in closer to Amelia. "You know my secret?" I raise my eyebrows, hoping she won't make me say it.

She looks confused for a moment, then her eyes widen. "Yes!" If you can yell a whisper, that's what she does.

I stare at her, trying to keep a straight face. I let another moment pass, then whisper, "Yes."

"No shit! Seriously?"

"Shh! Yes."

She grabs my arm and drags me toward the front door for privacy. "Tell me what happens! Who else shows up? Is there any drama? Does Trace love me?"

That last one catches me off-guard, and I immediately feel guilty because if I was really Amelia's best friend I should already know that this is what's on her mind. I tap the side of my head, pretending to think. "Several people I don't want here, yes, and I can't read minds. But," I pause dramatically, "if I had to guess, I would say yes."

She squeals and jumps up and down, holding my shoulders to keep from falling over and I end up jumping with her. "Do you really think so?" she asks, slightly out of breath.

"I'm no expert, but from the way he looks at you," I glance to where Trace is sitting at the island, looking a little lost, "and how lonely he looks sitting in the middle of all his friends while you're over here, I'd say it's definitely love."

Her face lights up. I don't think I've ever seen her so happy, so beautiful, and for the first time in a week my heart feels full again. Seeing my best friend so happy doesn't replace the hurt I'm still feeling from breaking up with Cameron, but it's close, and I'm suddenly grateful to Trace for bringing this out in her.

Amelia pulls me into a hug. "I've missed this. I feel like we never talk anymore."

"Me too." Her hair tickles my nose and I pull away just as the door swings open and Christina and her entourage walk in.

Christina gives me a once-over, then smiles at Amelia.

"Really?" I cross my arms and stand in the middle of the entryway to stop her.

She puts her hands on her hips and the other girls mimic her. "What?" The word is sharp, quick, and she emphasizes the T. It's probably meant to be intimidating but it reminds me of a little kid first learning to read, the way they sound out every letter.

I snort. "I mean, really, you think you're welcome in my house?"

Christina's mouth opens in astonishment and Amelia gives me a surprised look but doesn't say anything. On another day I might be hurt that she doesn't jump to my defense, but I'm still so pissed off about Christina's display in front of my dad that I don't need backup.

Christina looks past me to where Aiden is sitting in the kitchen, then looks back at me, her lips pursed. "All my friends are here. Why wouldn't I be?" She tosses her hair over her shoulder in a gesture of confidence but I can tell I rattled her.

I loop my arm through Amelia's and turn us away from the door. "Whatever," I say over my shoulder as we walk away. I would love to kick the bitch out, but Amelia still seems to like her and I don't want to cause problems now that we've made up.

"What was that about?" Amelia whispers.

"Let's call it preventative measures to keep her from being a royal bitch later." The adrenaline from standing up to her is fading and my hands start to shake. "I need food."

I'm inhaling another handful of chips when Nate, Katie, and Maddy arrive.

Time for round two.

Chapter 20

Christina's squeal makes everyone in the living room turn as the can of soda hits the ground. I scan the room before running to clean it up: Nate and Katie are settled into a corner, same as before, and so far no one has spilled anything on the floor.

In the kitchen, Christina stands over the puddle of soda, an amused smile on her face. She tilts her head but makes no move to clean it up. "My bad."

I grab a bunch of paper towels and shove them at her. "Here you go."

Christina's mouth opens in surprise. "But—"

I give her a once over, lingering on her feet, which are in the sticky mess. "You just said it was you, so here, clean it up."

She turns back to the island for support but finds none.

Amelia gives me a smile. "Come on, Christina. It'll take two seconds."

Her eyebrow furrows and she scowls at me. She leans closer and lowers her voice. "No one tells me—"

"Maybe you should be a little more careful." I thrust the paper towels at her hands and she finally takes them. I give her a fake smile and raise my voice an octave. "Thanks!"

Amelia snorts and a couple of the guys laugh, including Aiden.

Christina shakes the paper towels at me, her voice still low enough that the others can't hear her. "I won't forget this."

"I hope not. No one likes a mess on their floor."

Speaking of which, I need to check the living room again. I push past Christina, bumping her shoulder a little harder than I mean to, and step into the living room just as Nate tosses an empty can onto the coffee table, knocking several cups onto the floor. The kids from photo class on the couch all jump at once and in seconds a multitude of colors are seeping into the carpet.

My eyes move from the floor back to Nate, who's watching me over Katie's head. She's cuddled against his side, but her eyes are focused beyond him, like she's in another place and

Nate is just an escape from her everyday life. I wait for the smart-ass comment that I'm sure is coming, but he just stares at me. His gaze is more unnerving than his words. I shake off the creepy feeling that's snaking up my back and hurry to the kitchen for more paper towels.

Christina is sitting at the island, her arm looped through Aiden's. She did a half-assed job cleaning, but even that was more than I expected.

Back in the living room, I press a wad of paper towels to the largest puddle before moving on to the smaller ones. When I first started flickering I gorged myself on time travel movies, hoping to learn about my new ability. The biggest point of contention seemed to be whether or not you could change the future by doing things differently in the past. Some feared even the smallest variation could be catastrophic, undoing events that were the foundation of our society, blah blah, but others believe that small adjustments don't really make a difference, that if something is meant to happen—like someone dying or robbing a bank—it will happen despite a time traveler's intervention.

I fall somewhere in the middle. Katie is proof that my actions can change things for the better, but flickering to do better on tests totally backfired on me earlier this year when I got suspended. Situations like this party are a gray area for me. I stood up to Christina and made her clean up her own mess, but here I am, cleaning up after someone else. Different, but the same.

Nate's eyes burn into my skull and I finally look up to glare at him. "What?"

"Looks like you found your calling, freak."

I sigh.

"When you're done here I've got some carpet at my place you can do next."

My stomach drops. He's probably just talking crap. Why would he need to threaten me?

Katie giggles, but when she catches my eye her smile fades.

I sit back on my heels and wipe my hands on the front of my jeans. "If you hate me so much, why are you even here?"

Nate rests his hand on Katie's hip and she snuggles closer. "My girl here said you invited us. You saying we're not welcome?"

I cross my arms. "She is."

"That's how it is?"

"Yes."

He untangles himself from Katie and stands, taking a step closer to me. I scramble to my feet, not wanting him to have any advantage over me. We glare at each other, each waiting for the other to make the next move.

I'm done letting him push me around. "I think you should leave."

"Do you." It's a statement, not a question.

"Yeah." I glance over my shoulder to see if anyone's watching and lock eyes with Trace. Before I can blink out an S-O-S he's on his feet, touching Amelia's arm on his way to my rescue.

He looks between me and Nate. "What's going on?"

I wait, curious what Nate will say.

He glares at me. Katie pushes herself out of the chair and stands just behind Nate, but he doesn't seem to notice.

Trace waves a hand between us. "Hello?"

"Nate's an asshole and I asked him to leave." I wave my hand dismissively at him. "But he's still here."

"Dude, why do you want to stay someplace you're not welcome?"

Nate shrugs. "I was invited."

Trace doesn't move from his spot next to me, but his entire

body seems to grow larger, more menacing. "Now you're uninvited." He glances over his shoulder the same way I did moments earlier, and Heath and Aiden appear at his side, arms crossed over their inflated chests.

How do guys do that?

Nate seems to wither in front of us. "Whatever." He grabs Katie's hand and motions to Maddy on the couch. "There's a better party a couple miles from here."

He moves past me without a word, but Katie pauses in front of me, stopping him. "I thought you were my friend." Bitterness drips from her voice and I take a step back in surprise. "Thanks a lot."

They move through the crowd that has now gathered at the edge of the living room. When the door slams, everyone returns to their conversations.

I rub my arms. How did that go so badly? All I want is to keep Katie safe. I've stopped whatever happened in the bathroom, but what if it happens at the next party and I'm not there to help her?

Then another thought strikes me: since she just left, Cameron won't come here and we won't talk outside. But, I argue with myself, every other time I've flickered the basic thing still happens, even if I alter how it happens. Which means we'll still talk one way or another.

I slump onto the bottom step as yet another thought hammers me: Katie is still going to freak out, and what if this time she finds whatever it was she was looking for in the bathroom and manages to hurt herself?

My fingers touch my phone in my back pocket. I could text Cameron, but telling him that I kicked his sister and her demented boyfriend out of my party when I knew that something was going to happen might not go over very well.

Amelia sits next to me with a thump.

I raise an eyebrow at her. "That was so not like you."

"You don't look like you're in a full-body-tackle kind of mood."

"When has that ever stopped you?"

She leans against me so our shoulders are touching. "You okay?"

I take a deep breath and exhale slowly. "I think I've made things worse."

She moves her head closer to mine. "The flickering?"

"Yeah."

"Did something else happen with Christina?"

I'd nearly forgotten about her. "No. It's Katie."

"But they just left. I figured when you kicked them out that you were trying to change things."

"I was, but I didn't think it all the way through. When I repeat stuff I can change how things happen, but the actual events don't really change much. Like when I broke up with Robby. The first time he got really pissed and said a lot of mean things to me, so I flickered and altered our conversation. But we still broke up."

She's quiet for a moment, a faraway look in her eyes. "Some day you're going to have to tell me all the times you've flickered." She touches my arm. "But what happens with Katie?"

"I'm not sure about the details, but she and Nate were in the bathroom and she started screaming. He ran out of the house and Heath and Trace went after him and kicked his ass. I found Katie in the bathroom freaking out about how she'll never be able to be with a guy after what Turner did to her."

Amelia's face goes white. "Holy shit."

"Yeah."

"So did he..."

"Katie said no, that she wanted to be with him."

"But she freaked out because... man, she has a lot to deal with. I figured once she was rescued everything would be okay."

I think of Cameron and what he said about Katie refusing to go to the psychiatrist. Which I technically no longer know. "Far from it."

"So what are you going to do?"

"I'm considering texting Cam."

She leans back against the step and stretches her arms in front of her. "Eesh."

"But I can't decide if I should get into the details or just say 'you need to find Katie.'"

"I vote you don't freak him out with a cryptic text that'll make him think she's missing."

I laugh, but it's a sharp, bitter sound. "Good point."

She sits forward and rests her knees on her elbows. "Do you want me to help you figure out what to say?"

"No. Go find Trace and make out or something." I wink at her then slap her butt as she gets up. The playfulness fades as soon as she's gone, and I'm filled with dread. The sooner I get this over, the sooner Cameron can help Katie.

Me: Hey. I just kicked Katie & Nate out of my
party because I flickered & at the first party
something happened with them & she totally
freaked out. I'm afraid it's still going to happen, but now I can't help her. You need to
get her to go home NOW.

My fingers tremble as I rest my phone in my lap. This won't

go well.

Chapter 21

I'm still sitting on the steps waiting to hear back from Cameron when Christina and Aiden approach the stairs holding hands.

"I don't think so."

Christina narrows her eyes at me. "Who do you think you are?"

I stand so I'm blocking the stairs. "This is my house." I look at Aiden. "No offense to you, but you're not going upstairs with this skank."

My phone chooses that moment to buzz in my hand.

Christina glances at it before stepping closer to me. Her breath smells sickly sweet, like a combination of candy and alcohol. "I won't forget this."

I speak to Aiden. "Trust me, I'm doing you a favor." Then I face Christina. "One girl to another: you might want to find some mints before doing whatever it is you're planning to do."

Aiden laughs under his breath and Christina whirls on him, then snaps her head back to face me. "You little bitch!"

My phone buzzes again and she uses that moment of distraction to push me back on the steps. I fall awkwardly on my back and my phone clatters to the floor.

Aiden grabs Christina's arm and drags her away. "Let's go. My car is around the corner."

"Have fun!" I call after her in a fake-sweet voice before rescuing my phone. I take several deep breaths to settle my nerves but I'm too anxious.

I press the button.

> Cameron: Do you know where she went?
>
> Me: No. Nate mentioned another party near here.
>
> Cameron: Is Maddy with them?
>
> Me: Yeah.
>
> Cameron: We'll find them.

My heart drops into my stomach. I want to ask 'we, who?' but I already know. He's with Sarah.

Me: Will you tell me when you find her?

Cameron: Yeah. Thanks.

I start to type a smiley face but it's inappropriate for so many reasons, the biggest being that his sister is on the edge of a breakdown. No smiley face.

Me: Good luck.

I check the time on my phone before sliding it into my back pocket. It's barely eleven. Another hour to go before everyone has to leave.

The stains on the carpet aren't quite as bad as the first time, so I might get away with scrubbing the spots instead of renting a machine. This may end up being the only thing that went right tonight, and I'll be pissed if I get a migraine for saving the carpet. Quite a step down from saving little girls.

I join the group in the kitchen and wedge myself into a space between Amelia and a random girl I don't know. The mood is light, calm—much different from Heath's post-fight bravado. I guess I saved Nate from getting his ass kicked, too. For a short time I'm able to forget about Katie and Nate and even Cameron, losing myself in the laughter around me, for once not worrying about everything.

Amelia nudges me. "That looks good on you."

I look down at myself, not sure what she means. "What?"

She pokes my cheek with her finger. "Your smile."

A laugh bubbles up from somewhere deep inside me, and while it feels good to let it out, I fear it's the last one left inside me.

"Was tonight better than the first one?"

I run through a mental checklist. Nate is gone, Katie didn't freak out, Christina isn't in my bed. All good. But I didn't have that talk with Cameron. "Not as good as it could have been, but definitely better."

"That deserves a toast!" She shoves her half-filled cup into the space over the island. "Cheers!" The conversations around us stop and everyone raises whatever they're drinking, eyes on Amelia. "To Biz!" Their eyes shift to me, but for once the stares don't make me uncomfortable. Instead of the curiosity and confusion that so often follows me around, all I see is kindness and acceptance.

I raise my glass and we smash our cups together, spilling most of what was inside. After we've taken the obligatory sip—or gulp for the guys—I slide an arm around Amelia's waist and give her a hug. "Thank you."

"People love you, you just need to get over yourself to see it." I give her a puzzled look and she points at my head. "Like your hair. No one cares except you."

"Nate does."

"Only because it's so obvious that it bothers you."

"And Christina? The first time I met her she couldn't resist making fun of me."

"You were right. She's a bitch." She laughs. "But really she's just jealous. Not many people can rock the Sinead look like you."

I touch the side of my head. My curls are almost long enough to actually resemble curls—and tonight it's crunchy with the product Amelia forced on me. "I guess."

"Trust me."

My phone buzzes. "I'll be back. My butt's vibrating."

"Sounds like a good problem." Amelia winks, then presses closer to Trace.

I lean against the wall at the entrance of the living room and open my phone.

Cameron: I can't find her.

Cameron: She's not answering her phone.

Me: Can I do anything?

Cameron: I don't know.

Cameron: I can't drive around all night.

Me: Keep me posted?

Cameron: Yeah.

I picture him driving from neighborhood to neighborhood, searching for Nate and Katie without knowing what he's looking for. With Sarah in the seat next to him. No matter what I do, I keep throwing them together.

The group from my photo class vacates the couch, murmuring goodbyes as they walk past me. I move to where they were and flop onto the couch. Twenty more minutes. I need to get through another twenty minutes and then I can go to bed and forget this entire night.

Both of them.

That thought motivates me to clean up even though I know Amelia is going to give me the stink eye when she sees I'm cleaning instead of dancing on the coffee table.

Without the carpet stains the living room almost looks clean, even with the cups and candy wrappers. I stack up the empty cups and head for the trash can in the kitchen as a door opens upstairs.

Dad catches my eye and smiles. "Almost time to shut things down."

"Okay." I keep my reaction neutral so he doesn't realize how thrilled I am. I squeeze my way into the group at the island, cups still in my hands. "Hey guys, my dad just announced last call."

Technically last call means you have time for one more drink, but they know what I mean. Chairs squeak on linoleum as they move away from the island. Amelia presses her forehead to mine, a smirk playing on her lips. "You made it."

I laugh and give her a quick hug. "I did. Thanks for making me do this."

"Anytime." Her face grows serious. "Have you heard from Cam? Has he found Katie?"

"Not yet."

"I'll let you know if I hear anything." She waggles her phone in the air. "Gossip has a way of finding me."

"Thanks. Talk to you tomorrow."

I wave to Trace and call 'goodbye' as everyone files out of the house. I push the front door shut and turn the deadbolt, resting my head against the cool metal.

"Did you have fun?"

I turn around, still leaning on the door. Dad is sitting in one of the recently abandoned chairs at the island. "More than the first time."

His lips press together and his nostrils flare.

"I had to."

He crosses his arms. "Biz, you shouldn't be risking your health, especially not for something as silly as a party. You promised." He takes a breath. "I don't want you to end up like me."

"This was important. I stopped Katie from having a meltdown in the bathroom." I leave out the fact that I'm worried she might still freak out someplace else. I point at the living room. "The carpet isn't destroyed and I stopped a mean girl from funking up my bedroom."

He raises his eyebrow. "I'll have to trust you on that one. The carpet doesn't seem like a huge deal, but Katie? Is she okay? You haven't mentioned her much lately. Mom and I weren't sure how often you see her."

Where do I begin? "She's hanging out with some less-than-desirable kids at school, one of whom I kicked out of here tonight. Cameron said she refuses to see her doctor. Well, he technically hasn't told me that yet—he told me last night but we haven't talked about it this time."

Dad smiles. "That was always the most confusing part for me. Even the slightest change can prevent entire conversations from happening, but I still knew what was said. Got myself into more than a few tough spots that way." There's a faraway look in his eye and a sense of calm I don't often see.

"The one that stands out is when your mom told me she was pregnant with you. I flickered, and I was so excited I brought home a huge bouquet of flowers and sparkling wine, forgetting she didn't tell me until after dinner." He chuckles. "That took some creative talking. Lucky for me she bought it."

"You're sure she doesn't know?"

"I'm sure she suspects something, but she's never asked."

"Why not tell her? After all these years, especially with what it's doing to you now, don't you think she deserves to know?"

The smile slips from his face. "You're right. I've held this so close for so long that I guess I never realized it's okay to share."

I reach across the counter to touch his arm. "I think you should. Especially since you don't flicker anymore."

"But what about you? She'll see the similarities between us."

I hadn't thought about that. It would make my life easier if she knew, but once she makes the connection between Dad's illness and my flickering she'll have a whole new level of worry to deal with.

"I don't think we can tell her about me without also telling her about you. When you're ready, we'll do it together."

Since I promised to stop flickering, it really shouldn't be an issue, but part of me isn't sure I'll be able to quit cold turkey. "Dad, how did you stop?"

"I told you, I ended up in the hospital when you were born and decided it wasn't worth risking my health just to go back." He raises an eyebrow at me.

"Yeah, yeah, my health, I know. But that's not what I mean. I know why you stopped, but how did you stop." I pause, unsure of how to explain what I'm feeling. "Sometimes I'm so drawn to the light that it's hard to resist."

He flexes his fingers, as if recalling the first sensation. "Any time I got the urge, I looked into your crib and remembered why I stopped."

For a second my heart feels too big for my chest, but it's quickly withered by the fear that I'm not as strong as my dad.

That I can't live up to his example. "You make it sound so easy."

"It's not, but I'm here to help. In the meantime, I've decided I'd like to go with you to your next appointment with Martinez."

I stiffen. "Are you sure?"

"Deciding to stop flickering isn't that easy, so I'd like to do whatever I can to prevent this—" he waves his hands in front of his torso, "—from happening to you. When do you see him next?"

I pull out my phone to check my calendar. "Thursday."

His shoulders straighten and he nods once. "Then it's settled. We'll tell him then." He rises from the chair and carries a handful of trash to the bin.

"Dad, I've got it. Go to bed." I pull him in for a hug, burrowing my head under his chin like I did when I was little. He's bonier now, more frail, but when his arms wrap around me that same sense of security sweeps over me, like nothing bad could ever happen.

If only I could shake the feeling that everything is about to fall apart.

Chapter 22

Cameron's text comes just as I'm falling asleep.

Cameron: She's home.

Me: Is she okay?

Cameron: She's drunk. Parents are pissed.

I don't know how to ask more without freaking him out.

Me: How did she look?

Cameron: Hard to say.

I pause. He deserves to know what's going on with his sister, and I'm probably the person to tell him, but I'm afraid he'll shut me out even further.

Cameron: Can we talk tomorrow?

Me: Call in the morning?

Cameron: No, in person. Can we go to the
boat ramp?

My heart flutters. The boat ramp is 'our place'. We went there a lot when we first started dating, and it's where I told him about flickering. Is he ready to get back together, or is he ready to end things for good? Or, I remind myself, he wants to talk about Katie. Whatever it is, I promised I'd be there for him, and I will.

Me: Sure. 9am? Migraine coming around
10:30.

Cameron: Pick you up at 9.

Now my palms are sweating. I plug my phone into the charger and crawl under the covers. There's so much more I want to say—even stupid crap just to keep him texting me—but I don't want to push it. Hopefully tomorrow he'll say that he misses me and we can baby-step our way back together, but it's not going to happen tonight.

I sleep in fits. Even having the sheets instead of the bare mattress doesn't help. I keep picturing Katie in the bathroom, desperately searching for something to... all I can come up with is she wanted to hurt herself. And as good as it felt to kick Nate out of the party, I'm no longer sure it was the right thing to do. At least with Katie here at my house I could help her. Other people might not be as willing.

A rhythmic buzzing wakes me as the first hints of dawn streak across the ceiling. I stretch an arm out from beneath the covers and pull my phone underneath, hiding from the sun. The display is full of texts from Amelia.

> Amelia: Gossip alert! I just heard that Katie totally freaked out at some burnout's party not too far from your house.

> Amelia: She was screaming and Nate ran off all guilty. Some girls found her crying in a bedroom.

> Amelia: She left with that chick who came to your party with her.

> Amelia: Have you heard from Cam?

> Amelia: Are you still sleeping?

> Amelia: Call me.

I press the button to call Amelia, a thousand questions racing through my mind. Who told Amelia about Katie? Was she the same as she'd been at my house, or worse? Did Nate do anything?

"Oh good, you're up."

"Why are you up? It's barely light out."

Amelia giggles into the phone. "Trace just left."

I'm awake now. "This is new, right?"

"Mm-hmm."

"What about your parents?"

"They went out with friends last night, which means they sleep hard and late—" she emphasizes the last word, "—so I had him stay over."

I can hear her smile through the phone. "How was it? How are you?" Katie is still at the front of my thoughts, but I can spare the momentary distraction for my best friend. This is huge.

"I'm good. It was perfect. He's perfect."

My heart feels happier than it has in a long time. "I'm so excited for you, Amelia. He seems like he really likes you."

"Biz, he told me he loved me! I totally didn't expect it but he said it when we were making out in his car and that's pretty much when I decided to sneak him inside."

A spark of cynicism shoots through me, but Trace is a good guy. He wouldn't tell her that he loved her just to sleep with her. At least I hope not. "That's so great." My enthusiasm sounds fake, even to me, and Amelia doesn't miss it.

"What's wrong?"

"The stuff with Katie. I'm really worried about her. Did you get any details about last night?"

"Just what I texted."

"Flickering didn't help her."

"But you tried. That's all you could do."

"I know, but it wasn't enough. I keep thinking I should be able to do more. Cam texted last night when she got home but didn't say much. He's picking me up this morning to go to the boat ramp."

"Oh?" The suggestion in Amelia's voice makes me laugh.

"Nothing like that."

She snorts. "You never know."

"Oh god, now everything's going to be about sex, isn't it."

"Yep." She laughs. "Let me know how it goes."

"'Kay." I hang up and try to go back to sleep, but it's pointless. There is too much information bouncing around my skull. I head downstairs to make breakfast and finish cleaning up before Cameron arrives.

One benefit to an old car is I hear Cameron before he pulls into the driveway. As I'm reaching for the front door, an impulse hits me and I race to my room for my camera. I don't know how long we'll be out, but the light is always the best in the morning and I haven't taken pictures all week.

He doesn't get out of the car to open my door, but he does reach over and open it from the inside. Chivalry hasn't completely died just because we broke up. I get in and put my camera between my feet, messing with the strap longer than necessary so I can avoid looking at him. Knowing what he already said, what he's thinking about me, is making it hard to put a sentence together.

"Morning." He shifts the car into reverse and we're leaving my neighborhood before I find my voice.

"Hey." Brilliant. You'll win awards with that prose.

We ride in silence. I risk little glances at his fingers, the bit of wrist poking out of his sleeves, the curve of muscle in his leg visible even through his jeans, but the quiver in my stomach makes me turn away.

"You okay?"

"Yeah, just tired."

"How was the party?"

"Okay." It would have been a hell of a lot better if you'd been there.

"Sorry I didn't come, but..."

I let his words hang between us. I'm assuming he's still feeling what he told me the first time at the party, and I don't want to risk saying something stupid to prevent that from happening.

"Anyway, thanks for meeting me."

I finally look at him. When did things get so awkward between us? We've always been able to tell each other everything and now even a polite conversation is brutal. "Of course." I give up trying to talk until he pulls into the boat ramp parking lot. "Do you want to sit by the water?"

"Yeah." We climb out of the car and he grabs the blanket from the trunk. Memories of us curled up on that blanket, cuddled together, kissing, stop me in my tracks.

He notices. He holds up the blanket. "This okay?"

"Yeah, whatever." I walk ahead of him to the water's edge. Light dances over the water, which shimmers in the morning breeze. The blanket hits me in the leg and I turn. Cameron is holding one end and giving me an expectant look.

"Help me out?"

I reach for the corner and we stretch it over the already-flattened grass. We settle on opposite ends but the space feels more like two hundred feet than two. "So how's Katie?"

He sits cross-legged and puts his head in his hands, elbows on his knees. His normally strong shoulders are slumped in defeat and his fingers twist in his hair. "I don't know what to do. She was crying when she came home last night but she wouldn't tell me why."

"I think I know."

He turns his face to look at me, his head still resting on his hands. Sunlight catches the moisture in his eyes and my heart stills for a second. I hate seeing him hurt like this.

Where to begin? "I flickered yesterday because something happened at my party the first time." I give him the highlights, skipping over what Nate said to me. Cameron's jaw tightens as I talk, and his body goes rigid. "Last night Nate was being a dick, again, so I kicked him out before anything happened with Katie. Before they left she got really pissed at me and said she thought I was her friend and I felt like complete shit. Nate said there was another party nearby so they left with Maddy."

I pause when I say her name, but he doesn't say anything about Sarah. "At first I was happy that I stopped him from— well, stopped whatever happened—but then I started worrying that it would still happen, just someplace else, and that's when

I texted you." I take a breath and he smiles. "What?"

He's quiet for several minutes, his body still. "I miss you. This is the longest we've ever gone without talking."

Even though I knew this was coming, the ache in my chest grows stronger. "I know."

"So do you think whatever happened with Nate at your house happened again?"

I look at my hands. "I know it did."

He sits up straight. "Why didn't you say so?" He's close to yelling and I raise my hands to calm him down.

"I was getting there. You said you missed me and I lost my train of thought." His mouth opens in surprise and a blush creeps over my skin. I press my hands against my cheeks to cool them. "Amelia texted this morning. She didn't have details, but she heard that Katie freaked out at a party and Nate ran off without her, just like at my house. That's all I know."

His fingers clench into fists, then flex open, then back into fists.

"Kicking Nate's ass isn't going to solve anything."

"It would make me feel better."

"True. But Katie doesn't need more violence, especially not

from the people she trusts."

He rests his hands on the blanket, palms open. "Do you think she still trusts me?"

I take a quick breath, then spit out the words before I can think about it. "You're the most loyal and trustworthy person I know. She knows that you—we—care about her, you just need to find a way to get through to her. To make her realize she's not alone in this."

He plucks at a fold in the blanket. "Can you help me? I thought I needed to do this on my own, but you can see how well that's working." His eyes are in shadow, making them even darker than normal.

I wish I could tell what he's thinking. "You know that I love Katie and I've been doing my best to protect her. I feel responsible for her—like I brought her back to this."

"You did, and I'll always be grateful for that. Who knows what would have happened if you hadn't stopped Turner."

This isn't the time to share my growing suspicion that whatever was going to happen is still going to happen. "So how do we get Katie to understand that?"

He hangs his head. "I don't know."

We fall silent. The sun is higher now and my headache will be coming soon. Across the river a family of ducks—one mama and a dozen fluffy babies—swims along the shore, their bodies bobbing on the choppy waves. As they make their way along the water's edge, the mama suddenly quacks a series of urgent warnings, circling to the rear of the line so her babies are gathered into a tight circle. I unzip my camera bag and begin clicking.

A small red creature emerges from the foliage a few feet away from the shore. His pointy ears stand erect, one paw lifted as if he's deciding how to get the ducks.

"Fox," Cameron says.

I zoom in on his face—click-click-click—then shift to the mama and her babies. "I don't think I can watch this."

"Just keep taking pictures."

"But they're so little. Do they know he wants to eat them?" Click-click-click.

"It's part of their DNA. Fox bad. Mom good." I see him shrug from the corner of my eye.

The fox steps closer to the shore and the mama duck screeches louder. The babies move as one, a fuzzy brown and tan blob bouncing away from the shore, following their mother.

All except one.

I gasp as it continues along the shore, oblivious to its mother's cries and the fox, which has inched closer. "Cam, we have to do something."

His hand touches my knee and I jump. "It's nature. Survival of the fittest and all that. Besides, what are we going to do? By the time we get over there that duck'll be long gone." He removes his hand but I can still feel his heat where he touched me.

"You could throw a rock."

The fox crouches, his front feet in the water, nose just above the surface. Waiting. The duckling bobs closer, indifferent to its mother and now the added squawks of its siblings. The fox's tail lowers and his ears fall back in what must mean he's about to attack.

A splash startles the fox. He raises his head and looks past the duckling, but seeing no threat, lowers again. Another splash, this one a little closer, moves him backward. As if finally realizing what's going on, the duckling swims to its family, its tiny peeps carrying over the water. The fox watches from the shore, relaxed from his attack pose.

I lower my camera. Cameron is standing at the edge of the blanket, his hand full of rocks. My hero. "Can foxes swim?"

"Probably." He's still watching the fox, but it doesn't make another move toward the ducks, who have swum further away from the shore. Cameron looks so strong, so confident. The fear and uncertainty that have weighed him down in the months since Katie's return have slipped away, leaving the friend I fell in love with. That I'm still in love with.

I slide my camera into the case.

Cameron turns at the sound of the zipper. "Do you need to go?"

"Soon. But this is so nice I don't want to leave."

He tosses the rocks and lowers onto the blanket, closer this time. He doesn't touch me, but it doesn't matter. My heart is doing some kind of gymnastics, flipping and flopping so hard against my chest that I struggle to catch my breath.

I don't feel the same courage I did at the party, but I still have to ask. "So is this over?"

His eyes meet mine.

I know I shouldn't, but I lean closer.

"I don't want it to be."

The tears come faster this time and I press my eyes to keep them in check. The ball of pressure creeps up my throat.

"I've been thinking a lot. I care about you, that hasn't changed, but I need some time."

I swallow past the lump. "I'm not going anywhere."

In a quick movement he reaches over and squeezes my hand, but this time he doesn't let go. "I know."

Chapter 23

We're still holding hands when the headache hits without warning. My vision blurs for a second and I feel lightheaded, then blam! It's like a sledgehammer drives through my temple. I reach for my camera case as I slump over onto the blanket, hoping Cameron thinks I'm just messing with my camera, but he knows me too well.

He's on his knees leaning over me in seconds. "Is it bad? Should we go? We should go." He pulls me to my feet, then slides an arm around my waist. I tuck my head against his shoulder, inhaling deeply as if breathing him in can make me better. His arm tightens and he half-carries me to the car. I stumble over rocks, grass, clumps of dirt. I'd probably trip over a tree if he wasn't guiding me so carefully.

"You really fall apart when these things hit, don't you?"

I attempt a smile into his chest. "There's a reason I try to make sure I'm in bed."

He opens the car door with his free hand and guides me to the seat, leaning over me until he's sure I'm not going to fall out. My eyes are closed but I feel his breath on my cheek a moment longer than necessary, then his cheek as it grazes against mine as he clicks my seatbelt into place. "I'll go grab our stuff." His voice is hoarse, quieter than before, and my pulse quickens.

When he returns to the car he tosses the blanket in my lap. "Do you want that for—"

I drag it over my head before he can finish. "Thank you," I mumble from beneath my cocoon.

Hard as I try to quiet my thoughts, a million questions hammer me, pulsing in time with the hammering in my head. Is he looking at me? Is he thinking about holding my hand again? Did he hold my hand before out of gratitude, or because he wants to get back together? And then a quieter thought pushes the others away: how is Katie? I know she's home safe, but she seems to be getting more out of control every day.

After several turns the road levels out beneath us. My stomach tightens as we accelerate, then does a double backflip when Cameron laces his fingers through mine. His thumb traces small circles on the back of my hand, the looping rhythm matching the pounding of my heart. I try to focus on the heat of his skin, letting his warmth seep into me, warming me from the inside.

When the car stops he clears his throat. "Thanks for meeting me. I know I haven't really been fair to you the last week."

I pull the blanket off my head, blinking at the sudden brightness. My hand feels cool where he was holding it. "I'm glad we're talking now."

He reaches for my hand again. "Me too."

I want to sit here forever but I'm afraid I might throw up in Old Berta. "I need to go lie down."

He nods and I follow his gaze to our hands, which are resting on the edge of my seat. His other hand unfastens his seatbelt and before my brain can register what's happening, his lips are lightly brushing mine. Everything inside me threatens to break. I want to melt into him, to kiss him forever, but he pulls away, moving his face so our foreheads are touching. His free hand moves over my hair until his fingers touch the back of my neck, and he gently kneads the tense muscles. "Call me when you're able to talk."

I nod against his head, unable to stop the tears that slip through my lashes. "I will."

*****

The next morning the oppressive fog has lifted and I pop the camera card into my computer, anxious to see the pictures from the boat ramp. The progression from cute, fluffy duck family to potential horror show happens in an instant and I can't pull my eyes away from the fox. In the frames when he's by himself he's not very threatening, but the second the baby that got separated from its mom enters the picture the whole dynamic changes. I get a shiver up the back of my neck and over my head. These are good.

But how do I pick the best?

Turner's voice comes to me. "Use a critical eye. Adorable is great but it doesn't sell. Look for the story, the hidden emotion. The picture that makes people put down their coffee because they need to know what happens next."

My fingers freeze over the keyboard. I don't want to listen to him. He brutalized little girls—Katie—for years. He's a horrible, horrible person.

Yet he taught me everything I know about photography. Like it or not, his influence will always be a part of me. I just have to push aside who he was as a person and hold on to his instruction.

Time slips by as I scrutinize each photo. A knock sounds on the bedroom door, followed by Mom's voice. "You alive in there?"

"Come in." I smile as she opens the door. My stomach grumbles at the sight of coffee and toast.

"Thought you might be hungry." She pushes aside a pile of papers to make room for my breakfast, then leans over my shoulder. "Biz, these are amazing. When did you take them?"

"Yesterday. At the boat ramp with Cam." My stomach does a little flip and I take a sip of coffee to quell it. I continue scrolling and she rests her hand on the back of my neck. "I can't decide which one to submit. The close up of the fox and the baby duck shows a ton of detail, but the one that's pulled back to include the other ducks shows more of the story."

She gently kneads my neck. "Can you send in both? That's

why they have editors, right? To make those tough decisions?"

My fingers fly over the keys. "You're right. I'll send both." At the last moment I decide to include a third, and in seconds the pictures are traveling over the interwebs to the newspaper. I twist around to look at Mom. "Thanks. I would have sat here the rest of the day trying to choose."

"You're welcome. Why don't you come downstairs? It feels like forever since the three of us have spent time together."

"Okay. I'll be down in a minute." I activate the automated backup system on my computer, then grab my toast and coffee and head downstairs.

I sense an ambush the moment I step into the living room. Mom and Dad are side-by-side on the couch, matching cups of coffee on the table in front of them. Dad nods at the chair and I obediently sit.

I furrow my brows at Mom. She totally played me. "What's up?"

Dad begins. "College."

I sigh. "This again?"

"You haven't said a word about it since the last time we talked, so yes, this again."

Mom sits forward. "Biz, I know it feels like you have all the time in the world, but entrance deadlines are in a month and considering English isn't your best class, you shouldn't put the essays off until the last minute." She touches Dad's leg and he takes over. A literal tag-team.

"We understand why you don't want to go far from home, but will you at least look at state schools? Some are only an hour or two away." He looks down. "You could be home in a matter of hours."

I press my hands to my cheeks. I know they're right. I've always planned to go to college and I don't know why I've put it off. Aside from the whole catch-a-kidnapper-and-brain-surgery thing. That and the concern that instead of just worrying about what I'll be when I grow up, there's always the concern that one wrong turn down a sunny, tree-lined street could send me to the hospital. I ask a question that's been bothering me for weeks. "Is photography even a valid major?"

Mom smiles. "Yes. What else?"

"How will we pay for it? We're not exactly rolling in the dough, and I refuse to force a choice between me and Dad."

Mom continues. "There are scholarships, although if you

want those you really need to hurry up. Otherwise we'll look at financial aid. We can help some, but you'll have to bear the majority of the cost."

"But we don't want that to hold you back. You find the school you want to go to and we'll help make it happen."

I look back and forth between them. "I'm not going to win, am I?"

Mom leans back. "This is your future, Biz. You've had a lot to deal with lately, and even though it feels like the biggest thing you'll ever encounter, this will pass and there will be other challenges. We don't want you to feel like you missed an opportunity."

I take a long drink of coffee, thinking. Staying within driving distance would alleviate the guilt of leaving home. "Are state schools cheaper?"

They both smile and answer in unison. "Yes."

I slap my hands on the armrests, then stand up. "Well, I guess I have some research to do."

I'm contemplating the benefits of an urban campus versus one that's self-sustaining when I get an email from Shelly.

Biz these are AMAZING! We grouped all three so they tell the story and it's already on the website.

They'll be in tomorrow's paper, probably in the life-style section.

Can you stay after class tomorrow? I've been wanting to talk to you about what comes next—your plans for the future, that kind of thing.

Nice work!

Shelly

I stare at the email for a moment before opening a new tab for the paper's website. The first shot shows the entire scene—the mama and babies as the fox emerges from the brush—then it's a close-up of the baby drifting closer to the fox who's crouching at the shoreline, finishing with an even closer-up shot of the fox nearly lying on the ground, his tongue flicking over the side of his snout as he stares at the camera.

A smile plays over my lips. I did this on my own, without cheating. Right time, right place. I zoom in on the photo. I'd hoped they would use that one, but I wasn't sure how it could be presented since the ducks weren't in the shot. I never imagined they'd do a three-photo spread.

I grab my phone from the edge of the desk and text Cameron to check out the website, then click back to the tab with colleges. I've already missed the deadlines for early admission, but I can make the regular deadline if I get my act together. Maybe I can do this.

Chapter 24

Things change dramatically on Monday. No one ever emails me so I don't check my phone until I'm at my locker. "Fifty emails? Who the hell is emailing me?" The addresses all have some kind of newspaper name in them: herald, journal, chronicle, tribune. I click one in the middle of the bunch.

Dear Ms. Clement,

We absolutely love your pictures of the fox and the duck. Do you have more like this you'd be willing to send us?

Sincerely,

Dan Jones

Grand Traverse Herald

I click on another. It's the same as the first with one added line:

We pay $25 per published image.

"They pay?" Obviously professional photographers sell their photos, but I hadn't considered myself at that level. I look up and down the hall, feeling detached from the students around me. I'm still in a daze when strong arms wrap around me from behind.

Cameron nuzzles my neck, sending shivers through me, as well as a spark of uncertainty. Just like that we're back together?

I twist around, creating a small space between us, and hold up my phone. "Look."

He scans the email, his eyes growing wider. "They want to pay you?"

I nod, still a bit dumbfounded, both at him and the emails.

He scoops me into a bear hug and twirls me so my legs swing out from beneath me. People turn to stare but I don't care. He sets me down and we grin stupidly at each other.

"You're like a real photographer."

I duck my head. "I wouldn't say that."

He presses his forehead to mine. "I would."

"Twenty-five bucks hardly makes me a professional."

He grabs my phone and taps the screen before holding it up for me to see. "And how many emails do you have?"

I smile despite myself. "A lot." I don't know why it's so hard for me to accept success, however meager it may be.

"Yeah." He gives me another hug before glancing down the hall. "Want to grab some food after photography class today?"

"I can't. Shelly asked me to stay after to 'discuss my future'." I air quote the last part.

He pulls back. "What are your plans? I applied to State months ago."

"You did? How did I not know this?"

"That's what kids our age do. We go to school, eat fast food, sometimes drink when we're not supposed to, and apply to college. You haven't said anything but I assumed you had already applied."

I bite my lip. "No, not yet." This entire conversation feels forced. We weren't even speaking last week, and now it's like nothing happened?

"Apply to State. They don't have the best photography department but I don't plan to do that as a career."

"I looked at a few online yesterday..." I sound pathetic.

"Well get on it. You don't want to stay here forever, do you?"

"I'm not sure." My phone dings. Grateful for the distraction, I check as another ten emails come in. Too much is happening all at once. I lean an arm against my locker to steady myself.

His warm eyes hold mine before he cracks a smile. "I'm dating a superstar."

I swat his arm, pushing him away. "Shut up. I'll see you later."

Later turned out to be a couple dozen emails later and a bazillion texts from people who saw my pictures online. When I open the door to the newspaper everyone inside stands up and claps, including the people who work at the paper and aren't paid to pad the egos of a bunch of high school kids.

"This is insane," I mumble as I hurry to the table in the back of the room.

Shelly holds up her arms, hands in the air. "Woman of the hour!"

"Yeah, yeah." I pick an empty chair and hope the table will swallow me whole. Fortunately Shelly notices my embarrassment and starts class without any further comment.

Well, almost.

Toward the end of class she holds up the paper to show us my photos. "One of the key things you're taught about photography is that you should be able to tell an entire story with one image, that it shouldn't require any copy to explain what's going on. But—" she points at the paper, "—there are always exceptions. Biz did tell the entire story with one image. The first one shows the family of ducks and the one duckling that strayed too close to the fox, who's hungry for his next meal. End of the story, right?

"The second image focuses on the duckling and the fox, the epitome of survival of the fittest. Most people would assume the duck is in its last minutes. End of story.

"Then there's the final shot. When the subject is looking at the camera, we the viewer are brought into the picture. Without the other photos we don't know his prey is in front of him and we become the potential prey. It's a dynamic that's hard to achieve in nature and this photo does it exceptionally well."

Several heads turn my way and the familiar blush warms my face. Can they tell from the look on my face that bringing the viewer into the photo was the last thing I was thinking about when I took the pictures? I glance at Cameron, but judging from the proud smile on his face, he'll never give me away. And I'll never tell that I made him throw rocks to scare away the fox.

Shelly continues. "We decided to use all three images because, aside from all three being phenomenal photos, the story they tell together is greater than any of them on their own."

My phone buzzes in my pocket. I pull it out.

Cameron: That'd be $75.

I smile.

Me: Dinner's on me.

Cameron: I'm holding you to that.

I set my phone facedown on the table and look up to see Shelly watching me. I mouth 'sorry' but she just smiles and places the newspaper on the edge of the table.

"That's it for today. Using Biz as inspiration, this week I'd like you to take a series of photos, minimum of three, that can stand alone but together tell a bigger story. The subject is completely up to you." She moves around the table toward me as chairs squeak on the linoleum floor. Cameron catches my eye and winks, then turns and leaves with the rest of the class.

Shelly settles into the chair next to mine. "I'm sorry if I

embarrassed you, but you need to get over your inability to accept a compliment. I figure if you keep taking kick-ass pictures and I keep talking about them in class, by the time this year's over you'll learn to accept the praise you deserve." Her dark hair falls into her eyes as she waits for my reaction, but all I can think about is how much I'd love to have her hair. Maybe when it grows back it'll come back straight.

"Biz?"

"Sorry. I'm excited about this, I really am. I just have a lot on my mind lately." I straighten my shoulders, determined to stay focused on Shelly. "Turner said the same thing about me accepting compliments, but every time someone says anything nice I figure they're just saying that to be polite."

"This business is very competitive. One thing you'll discover very quickly is people are more likely to rip you apart than build you up." She reaches for a piece of paper in the middle of the table and scribbles something. "I should probably cover rejection with you guys." She looks me in the eye. "Some photographers will go their entire lives without any success. Some may even wonder if they have a right to call themselves photographers. But you have an excellent eye for composition and the way you use the light and shadow..." She trails off.

I've heard this before too. I credit it to my whacked out relationship with light. I'm always aware of its presence, of how it affects everything it touches, and I know the instance it shifts.

"I don't want to inflate your ego so much that you forget that this takes work, but I'm learning that you need an extra push to realize your potential."

I sigh. "That seems to be a running theme."

She tilts her head and her hair falls the other way. "Oh?"

"Yesterday my parents ambushed me about college."

Her eyes widen. "You weren't planning to go?"

"I am..." Where do I even begin? "My dad's sick and I don't want to be too far from home."

She leans back in her chair and exhales slowly, thinking. "What about state schools? How much have you researched?"

"Not a ton. I found a design school yesterday that sounds amazing, but it's not in-state and it's not cheap. With my dad's medical bills I don't see how it would work."

"There are always ways to pay. Financial aid, scholarships. If we start now I'm sure we can find a scholarship—maybe more than one—that would offset the cost. Student loans suck, believe me, I'm still paying mine, but they're a way to get the future you deserve."

I smile. "You should be a motivational speaker."

She doesn't miss a beat. "What do you think I do when I'm not here?" Her eyes soften and I feel like I could tell her anything. "Do you have a portfolio? According to the syllabus it looked like Turner was working toward that before," she waves her hand. "Well, you know. You'll need a portfolio if you're applying to design schools." She nods at the paper. "Actual clips from publications are huge, so the more you can get the better. Have you submitted to any regional papers?"

I hang my head. "I meant to."

"Biz, this is project numero uno. Believe me, I'd rather hang out with my dreamboat boyfriend, too—"

She thinks Cameron is a dreamboat?

"—but the next few months need to be focused on photography."

"This would probably be a good time to mention that my email has exploded today, huh?"

"What?!" She nearly shoots out of her seat. "You should have told me this before class. Who have you heard from?"

I open the email app on my phone and show her my inbox.

227

Ten more have come through since I last checked.

She scrolls through the list, nodding and smiling. On a couple her mouth falls completely open. Our eyes connect as she hands me my phone. "This is huge."

"A couple offered to pay for more photos."

"Biz, this is fantastic. You know what I said about getting used to compliments?"

I nod.

"It starts now."

Chapter 25

Amelia and I are walking to the cafeteria when the captain of the football team pauses to give me a high five.

Amelia stops in her tracks, mouth hanging open. "Strange things are afoot at the Circle K."

"Tell me about it."

"This is all from the fox pictures?"

"Yeah. Apparently I'm a hit on the internet." Part of me keeps waiting for this to turn into an elaborate prank, but the photos keep spreading online and more papers have asked for new stuff.

"I did see a meme with the one where he's looking at you."

"Seriously?"

"Yeah, but it was stupid, otherwise I would have shared it."

"Still, that's pretty cool." The line for the cafeteria is so long it's snaking into the hall.

"Can't you use your influence to cut?"

I snort. "Hardly."

"You never know if you don't try."

"Did I tell you some places want to pay me for more photos?"

Amelia smacks my arm. "Get out! How much?"

"Not a lot. Enough to put gas in my car."

Cameron's deep voice startles me. "Yeah, if she's driving cross country once a week."

I roll my eyes. "Whatever." Shelly's comment about learning to take compliments comes to me and I take a deep breath. "Thanks."

Amelia tilts her head. "For what?"

I poke her forehead. "For being so excited for me. Someone pointed out that I need to stop deflecting when people are happy for me."

Cameron drapes an arm over my shoulder. "That someone sounds smart."

A tiny twinge of jealousy pricks my chest. First Shelly calling Cameron a dreamboat and now he's calling her smart? Amelia notices the shift in my mood and narrows her eyes, but I shake it off. 'Nothing' I mouth. I told her over the weekend that things were back on with Cameron but I guess it's obvious things aren't back to perfect, at least not yet.

Instead of waiting in awkward silence, Amelia launches into a lengthy description of the movie she and Trace saw over the weekend. She doesn't stop until we're paying for our food.

Cameron pecks me on the cheek. "I'm gonna sit with the guys today. I'll see you in class."

"See ya." I watch as he walks to his old table and slides in between Double J—our inseparable friends Jason and Justin.

"So what's up? I thought the lovefest was back on?" Amelia takes a bite of greasy pizza, then sets it down, her nose wrinkled in displeasure. "I don't know why I keep getting this."

"Because you know how delicious pizza is supposed to be." I try to smile, but my heart isn't in it. "We didn't really talk about the reasons we broke up. We hung out and said we missed each other, then kissed."

She cracks a shit-eating grin. "Who needs talking when you can make out?"

I throw my napkin at her. "Shut it. I want to be with him, but I still don't know what was —or is—going on with Sarah.

Then our photography teacher Shelly made a comment about him being dreamy."

"Well he is."

"I know, but don't you think it's weird that a grown woman would say something like that?"

She shrugs. "I don't know. Maybe she was just trying to get you to open up. You obviously think he's dreamy." Her eyelashes flutter and she clasps her hands in front of her chest. "She probably thought that was the best way to get through to you. Did she follow it up with anything serious?"

I pick at my own pizza. "Yeah, she wanted to talk about my future, college and photography and all that."

Amelia throws up a hand. "See! That's all it was. Now quit worrying about her and tell me what's going on with that." She points at Nate, who's walking into the cafeteria. For a moment I'm surprised he doesn't have any bruises, then I remember that the guys beat him up at the first party, not the second. He sits with a couple of juniors, never dropping the cocky attitude.

"As far as I know Nate and Katie are together, or at least she follows him everywhere. I'm worried about her, and Cam said they don't know what to do. She refuses to go to her therapist but clearly things are not okay with her." I glance at Cameron to see if he noticed Nate's entrance and my breath catches in my throat at the mix of emotions on his face: anger, pain, frustration.

Amelia follows my gaze. "Do you think he'll do anything to Nate?"

"He wants to, but I pointed out that it wouldn't help things with Katie."

Cameron pushes back his chair and stands, fists clenched at his side.

"I'm not sure you convinced him."

Cameron's moving toward Nate's table and I'm out of my seat and weaving through the tables, angling so I'll cut him off before he gets to them. I grab his arm. "Cam, stop."

He whirls around. His dark eyes are nearly black and every muscle in his body is tense, ready for a fight. "How can he just sit there like nothing happened?"

"I don't know, but this isn't the way to find out." Pieces of Friday night—the first Friday night—flash through my mind. Katie on her knees rummaging through the drawers. Her tears as she said how Turner ruined her. "Katie's dealing with a lot and having her brother beat up the guy she likes, even if he is a complete asshole, is only going to push her away more. Talk to her after school. Tell your parents to drag her back to the doctor. But don't cause a scene in front of the entire school. That's just gonna push her even further away."

His fists relax and he exhales slowly, but his eyes never leave Nate. "I don't get why you're protecting him with the way he treats you."

Join the club. "It's not about him. It's about Katie. She needs to feel normal and as much as it sickens me, he's giving that to her."

He looks at me, but his eyes are still filled with hatred.

I take a half-step back. "Let it go. At least until after school."

"Fine." The anger fades but his mind is focused elsewhere. "I'll see you later."

I touch his arm as he heads back to his table and my hand falls limply to my side. When I turn back to my table Amelia's staring, unblinking.

"I stopped him from making a scene. For now."

Amelia takes a bite of pizza and shakes her head. "Even an internet celebrity can't save Nate from getting his ass kicked. It's only a matter of time."

I watch as Cameron and his friends look over their shoulders at Nate. Whatever plan they're coming up with is not going to end well.

For anyone.

Chapter 26

After school I make the decision to push Nate and Katie and Cameron out of my head and concentrate on myself. Shelly's excitement over the response to the fox pictures was the kick in the butt I needed to finally do something for my future, and I'm not wasting any time.

I pull up the schools I found in my first search after talking with Mom and Dad and click through to the application pages. The basic information is easy enough, but the essays will take longer. We've been writing sample essays in English class since last year, but I can't come up with a unique story that will impress the admissions people.

At least not one that I'm willing to tell.

My enthusiasm wanes when I realize I'll need Mom to write checks for the applications. I really wanted to get this done all in one night, and I can already hear her teasing me about wanting instant gratification. I save the half-filled applications and switch over to my email. More than 100 people from all over the country emailed asking for more photos, and I haven't replied to a single one. "Not the best way to start a career," I murmur. I open the first email, ready to type, but my words fail me. I can barely accept a compliment in person—how do I say it in an email?

Maybe I should focus on my pictures instead.

Half an hour later I'm flipping between five photos, unable to decide which is the best. I'm tempted to stop—to go watch TV or something—but another burst of motivation keeps me in my chair. I have a faint recollection of a tip sheet on application essays from English class, so I tackle the pile of papers that were sent to me after I had surgery, searching for anything helpful, but it's not there.

Back on the computer, I type "college entrance essays" into the browser search field and scroll through the sample questions until I find one that clicks: Some students have a background or story that is so central to their identity that they believe their application would be incomplete without it. If this sounds like you, then please share your story.

I may not be able to write about flickering, but I can write about the fear of following in my dad's footsteps. I sit straighter in my chair. That's totally it. I open a new document and my fingers get a life of their own. Apparently I just need a topic that interests me to be able to write a coherent sentence.

Twenty minutes later I hit print and lean back in my chair. I've done all I can on my own. Printout in hand, I head downstairs.

Dad's at the kitchen island reading the newspaper. He eyes the paper clutched in my hand. "What's that?"

I smile. "My college application essay."

His eyebrows shoot up.

"Will you read it?"

"I've been waiting for you to ask for my help." He pushes the newspaper aside and reaches for my essay.

My story is unique in how boring it is. My parents are happily married and would do anything for me. I've lived in the same town—even the same house—my entire life and I've had the same best friends since elementary school. But the one thing that most kids my age haven't experienced is that for most of my life, I've been waiting for my dad to die.

The first time I witnessed him seizing was in the monkey house at the zoo. I didn't understand what was happening—all I knew was my dad was hurt and my mom was screaming as loud as the monkeys.

Since then I've done whatever I can to make his life easier. I count out his daily pills, I try to keep the house clean, and since he hates technology, I don't make him touch my computer unless it's absolutely necessary. He, in turn, gives me his unconditional love and support. Together we appreciate the beauty of the world around us—me with photography, him with finding joy in everyday things.

I know he'll die long before my friends' parents, but what scares me the most is knowing my fate might be the same. I've already had one brain surgery but it hasn't changed anything. My biggest hope is that I can solve the puzzle that is my brain before it's too late.

My plans for the future aren't noble—I don't have lofty goals of becoming a doctor to cure myself. Instead I'm following the path that makes me happiest: photography. If I can spend my time capturing the moments my dad loves, then I'll know I've done something right.

I pick at my fingernails until he finally looks up. "It needs to be longer."

He clears his throat. "I think it's perfect."

"You don't think it's, I don't know, too desperate? Like, 'ooh, I've got drama, pick me, pick me'?"

He sets down the paper. "Quite the opposite. You've managed to demonstrate all your good qualities, including not making me use your computer."

I smile. "Not so fast. I still need to pick my best photos."

"For the application?"

"No, for the other newspapers."

He gives me a puzzled look and I realize I'm jumping all over the place.

"Sorry. I'm doing two things at once—applying to colleges and submitting photos to some of the newspapers who wrote about the fox pictures."

"Why don't you send each paper a different photo? Then you don't have to choose the absolute best one."

I throw my arms around him. "You're a genius!"

"I have my moments."

I pull away and look him straight in the eye. "Now about the essay. You don't think I need to change it?"

"Not a word. And as an added bonus you've further convinced me that telling Dr. Martinez is a good idea."

Chapter 27

"You're sure you want to tell him?"

"Biz, you've asked me a hundred times. Yes, I think we should tell him."

It's a few minutes before my appointment with Martinez and Dad hasn't stopped fidgeting since we sat down in the waiting room. My phone has buzzed a couple times but I ignore it.

"Even though you've gone your entire life keeping this a secret?" Deep down I agree that clueing Martinez in to the secrets of my head is probably a good thing, but this is different than telling my closest friends. He's a doctor. He's gone to school for eons—even if he doesn't look like it—and isn't going to swallow this as easily as Cameron and Amelia did. "You're one hundred percent sure?"

He grabs my hand. "No, I'm not one hundred percent sure, but he's your best chance to figure out why this happens to us. And to stop it from killing you." His lips tighten into a thin line. He squeezes my hand and holds it until the nurse leads us back to Martinez's office.

"Biz. Mr. Clement. How are you?" Martinez rises from his rolling stool to shake Dad's hand, then sits back down. Dad takes the chair near the door while I hop onto the examining table. The paper cover crinkles as I get comfortable.

Martinez rolls so he's facing me and clicks on a small flashlight. I widen my eyes and focus past his shoulder while he checks my pupils. "Looks good. When was your last headache?"

I glance at Dad before answering. "Saturday."

Martinez turns off the flashlight and grabs his notepad. "Did you write down the possible triggers?"

"Not exactly."

He lets out an exasperated sigh. "Biz, I can't treat you if you don't take this seriously. You get debilitating headaches but you won't avoid the triggers. There's no pattern to when they hit, yet you don't seem to care."

I finger the paper sheet, avoiding his gaze. "It's not that I don't care..."

He slaps his open palms on his knees and I look up. It usually takes longer for him to get this frustrated with me. "Then what is it?"

I lock eyes with Dad, who nods once before closing his eyes.

Martinez notices the exchange and faces Dad. "Sir, forgive me for being so blunt, but I can't give your daughter the care she needs if she won't disclose all the details." He turns his focus back to me. "Biz, what aren't you telling me?"

I take a deep breath, tilting my head back so I'm staring at the ceiling. "I know why I get headaches."

"Yes, I've figured that out."

"It has to do with sunlight." I lower my gaze to meet his eyes. "You know how when you're driving and the light flickers through the trees so it makes a kind-of strobe light effect?"

Martinez leans forward so his elbows rest on his knees. "Yes. You've mentioned before that the light bothers you."

Dad and I both smile. "I wouldn't say it bothers me so much as completely screws with my head."

"Biz," Dad reprimands.

"Sorry." I clear my throat before continuing. "The light does something to me. First my fingers and toes start to tingle, like when they fall asleep when you've been sitting in the wrong position for too long, then this crushing weight falls over me."

Martinez scribbles furiously in his notebook. He nods. "Go on."

"After what feels like minutes but is really only a couple seconds, the weight lifts and I feel like I'm floating."

"You get light-headed?"

"No."

He stops writing and watches me, waiting.

"After that..." I pause.

Dad sits forward in his chair. "Go ahead, Biz."

I close my eyes. "After the floating feeling, everything goes black for a split-second and then I go back to yesterday."

"Yesterday," Martinez repeats.

"Yes."

"I don't follow."

The relief I thought I'd feel doesn't come. He doesn't get it. Maybe this was a mistake.

"Biz, why don't you elaborate?" Dad asks.

Martinez looks between the two of us, his normally serious

face openly confused.

"I go back to yesterday," I repeat.

"Like déja vü?"

"Sort of, except I actually go back to the day before."

Martinez watches me, unblinking, before rubbing his hand over his face. "What you're talking about isn't possible."

Dad clears his throat. "It's quite possible."

Again Martinez's head swivels between us. His gaze settles on Dad. "Did she put you up to this?" Then back to me. "Biz, I know these appointments aren't your favorite but I don't have time for this."

I slap my hand on the table and the paper tears. "I'm telling the truth. Silly me thought you'd be excited to help us figure out why this happens, but I guess I was wrong." I slide off the table and step toward the door. "I don't have time for this."

"Biz, wait." Martinez catches me by the elbow, his hand warm through my shirt.

I turn to face him.

"Please sit back down. Did you really expect me to swallow this that quickly?"

I look at his shoes. Blue and orange running sneakers. "No,

I guess not." Then I look at his hand, which is still on my arm. My eyes dart to Dad, who's watching us with furrowed brows. Martinez drops his hand and I climb back onto the table.

Martinez sits on the stool and rests his notepad on his knee. "Let's try this again. And please don't just say that you go back to yesterday."

"But that's what happens. Before the surgery I would always go back eighteen hours, but now it's a full day."

"And you actually repeat the previous day. It's not a flashback or hallucination." These aren't questions. He's in analytical mode now.

Dad gives me a tight smile and nods for me to continue.

"Right. I repeat everything." Except for the things I change.

Martinez finishes writing then rubs his hand over his eyes again. "I'm sorry. Can we back up? You said the flickering sunlight makes this happen?"

"Yes."

Dad crosses his arms over his chest. "It's similar to a seizure. Once it starts there's very little we—she can do to stop it."

I smile as I remember all the stupid ways I've tried to stop flickering. Occasionally a big hat would work, but the only surefire way was to stick my head beneath the dashboard of the car, which left a lot of explaining to whoever is driving.

Martinez looks at Dad. "You believe this?"

"I do."

For a moment I wonder if he's going to confess that he flickers, too, but he doesn't continue.

Martinez opens his mouth to respond, then closes it. He focuses on me. "Aside from the tingling sensation, heavy weight, and lightheadedness, what are the side effects?"

"Nothing until I get back to the time that I flickered. That's when the migraine hits."

"So all this time you've been seeing me, you've known what causes your headaches?"

I nod.

"What effect did the surgery have?"

"It made me flicker further back by a few hours. At first I thought you fixed me. I avoided the places where I knew I could flicker because I didn't want to think about it. I was upset that just when I figured out that I could help people, my ability was taken away. About a month after the surgery Mom was driving me home from school and took a different route than normal. We drove through The Strand and—"

"The Strand?"

"It's a stretch of really tall, really straight trees. I can flicker there pretty much any time of day as long as there's sunlight."

Martinez nods, but I can't tell if he believes me.

"So anyway, I discovered by accident that I could still flicker. I've tried not to do it as much as I was before, but sometimes things happen that I have to fix. Like on Friday."

"You're telling me you can choose when to flicker."

"Yes and no." I think back to the day I stopped Turner. Cameron and I had to drive for miles to get out of the storm that had engulfed our town. "If the sun isn't out, I can't flicker. Depending on what I need to go back for, I can miss the window to get there in time. Mornings are usually the best."

He looks at Dad. "And you believe her?"

Dad smiles. "Yes."

"How did she convince you?"

"That's a story for another time."

Martinez rises from the stool, seeming to accept Dad's explanation—for now—and paces the small room. "Do you ever flicker by accident?"

"Not as much as I used to. The migraines are good motivation to try to stay in the present. Over the years I've figured out how to avoid the effects."

"How old were you when this started?"

"Thirteen."

"And where do you go when you flicker?"

I smile. His doctor brain is fighting this, but he's trying to understand. "Before the surgery, when I'd flicker eighteen hours, I'd sometimes end up in class, but now I come to wherever I was twenty-four hours earlier. Every now and then I'm in the bathroom, which is my favorite because then I have a minute to get my bearings before I see anyone. The worst is eating because I always choke."

Dad chuckles softly, but his eyes are far away, like he's remembering his own stories.

Martinez continues. "Bear with me. I'm doing my best to digest this." He checks his notes. "So once you flicker, you repeat everything that already happened?"

"Pretty much. I can change things—that's usually why I go back—but most of the conversations and other stuff stay the same." I think of Katie and how my attempts to protect her pushed her away further. "Lately I've realized that if I stop something from happening, it will eventually happen anyway. The thing with Turner was the only big thing that turned out well."

Martinez looks at Dad, then back at me. "Turner, your photography teacher?"

I nod.

"What did you have to do with that?"

I take a breath as memories of that day flood through me. "I'm the one who stopped him."

Chapter 28

Martinez shakes his head. "Turner was caught by an anonymous tip to the police."

Dad raises his hand. "Anonymous."

Martinez looks back and forth between me and Dad, brows furrowed. "How did—what did you have to do with his arrest?"

I take a deep breath and launch into the story. The picture I took of the little girl at the park, seeing on the news that evening that she'd disappeared, then flickering so I could keep her safe. Encountering Turner at the park and being drugged, then flickering out of his van. "That's when I told Dad everything and he called the police."

"Because Biz flickered back to the day before Turner took her, and two days before he snatched the little girl, all I could tell them was that there were girls at Turner's house." Dad's expression softens as he looks at me. "Fortunately it was enough. Then I made sure Biz was in the hospital before her headache hit."

A light seems to go off in Martinez's head. "That's when you had surgery."

I nod.

"You could have killed yourself."

I nod again.

"Huh." The corner of Martinez's mouth turns up in a smile. "I guess I need to give you more credit. All this time I figured you were drinking too much soda or not getting enough sleep, when really you're our own superhero."

"I wouldn't say that."

Dad clears his throat. "And you won't say that, right?"

"He can't because of the whole doctor-patient privilege thing."

Martinez smiles. "That applies to lawyers, but yes, your health and all the details surrounding it are confidential, unless you give me permission otherwise."

Dad's eyes go wide and I shake my head. "Dad, stop

worrying. I told you we can trust him." I look at Martinez. "Right?"

He straightens the notepad on his knee. "Of course you can trust me." The excitement in his eyes lights up his face in a way I've never seen. If only I could read his mind to know what he's not saying. "Now I have more questions."

I smirk. "I thought you might."

Half an hour later Martinez has filled a dozen pages in his notebook and my voice is scratchy from talking. I slide off the table and he stands at the same time, stepping close to me. "Biz, if what you're telling me is true, this is extraordinary."

"What do you mean if what I'm telling you is true? Why would I make this up?"

He shrugs. "Biz, I like you." He glances at Dad. "And sir, you seem like a perfectly nice man, but I'm a scientist, and frankly, all this..." he waves the notebook. "It sounds a little too fantastic to be true."

I push my shoulders back. "I can prove it."

Dad stiffens in his seat. We didn't discuss this, but I'm overwhelmed with the need for Martinez to believe me.

Martinez lowers the notebook. "How?"

My phone buzzes in my back pocket and I reach for it out of habit. Then a thought strikes me. "I can use my phone to record my face. As long as I'm still holding it when I flicker, the phone will travel with me and the recording should still be there." I feel kind of stupid for never thinking of this before.

He stares at my phone in my hand. "I don't want you further jeopardizing your health just to make a point."

I hold up the phone and smile. "But what if it's a fantastic point?" I can't resist twisting his words around. He's not the only one here with a grasp of the English language. "I won't flicker just to record it. I'll wait until there's a good reason."

Martinez shakes his head. "I'm not ready to agree to this. Doing so would mean admitting that I find your story valid, so right now I'll just say that I'm intrigued. If you bring me a recording, I'll take a look. Assuming this is okay with you, sir." He glances at Dad over his shoulder before his dark eyes find mine again.

"That's her decision. Biz, as long as you're comfortable I have no problem with you doing this. As you said, it's a matter of saving your life."

Martinez looks at Dad longer this time, as if trying to sort out a puzzle. We haven't told him that Dad used to flicker or the consequences it brought, but he's a smart man and he'll eventually figure it out. For now I want to keep him focused on me.

Which doesn't seem to be a problem. Martinez grabs my hand and clutches it between his. "Thank you for trusting me." The excitement in his voice, his eyes, his entire body, is contagious and I feel like I'll burst from smiling so hard.

I notice new details about Martinez—stubble darkening his jaw, which is clenching and unclenching, little flecks of hazel in his otherwise chocolatey brown eyes, a small scar on the bridge of his nose. Dad clears his throat and suddenly I'm aware of how close we're standing. His energy tugs at me but I release my hand and take a step back.

Martinez sets his notebook on the counter and moves to the door. "Are weekly appointments too often? I don't want to keep you from your studies, but we have a lot of work to do."

"Sure, that's fine."

"Let's schedule Thursday afternoons. Then you have Fridays free to do teenage things."

I suddenly feel awkward and don't know what to say. Whatever spell he cast on me as I answered his questions is broken and I'm left feeling empty.

Dad seems unsettled, too, but I don't ask about his concerned look until we're back in the car.

"Okay, what?"

"What?" Dad repeats.

"You obviously don't approve of something. What is it?"

He waits until I maneuver the car onto the main road before speaking. "Dr. Martinez seemed really excited."

"He's a neurosurgeon, what did you expect?"

"I don't know. More skepticism."

"He questioned me for half an hour!"

"Are you sure we can trust him?"

"It's a little late for that." But there's still something unspoken hovering between us. "Is something else bugging you?"

"I guess I hadn't realized how close you've become with Dr. Martinez. I know you've had a lot of appointments with him but..." he trails off.

I feel twitchy, like I've been busted doing something wrong, but I haven't done anything wrong, have I? "What are you getting at?"

"I understand that he's young and you've been working closely with him since the surgery, but if you ask me, his bedside manner is a little too chummy."

I think back to my last appointment when I collapsed and we ended up sitting on the floor. That could definitely fall into the "too chummy" category, but I collapsed. What was he supposed to do?

"Is he always so close to you?"

"Dad, he has to examine my head. Is he supposed to do that from across the room?" A new fear prickles my neck. Martinez is my best chance at finding out why I flicker. I can't let Dad take that away from me. Whatever uncertainty I feel about whether or not something inappropriate happened, I can't let Dad know. "I promise he's always professional. We dumped something huge on him today. I'd be worried if he wasn't excited." I watch from the corner of my eye to gauge his reaction.

"I suppose. But be aware of your boundaries. A grown man—even your doctor—should not be holding your hand and gazing into your eyes."

"He wasn't gazing."

"I'm not trying to put you on the defensive. I'm just asking you to be cautious."

"Fine. I promise not to fall under the captivating trance of

Dr. Martinez."

Was he gazing? I admit we were a little close, and maybe he was staring into my eyes for a moment too long, but he was just excited. A little voice whispers that I would be upset if I saw Cameron and Sarah like that, but I brush it off. Martinez is an adult. Nothing is happening with him.

The rest of the drive is silent. Once we're safely in the driveway I hop out of the car, but Dad doesn't move. I open the passenger door and study him. "Are you okay?"

"I just need a minute." He waves his hands in front of his eyes. "Being in the light, it affects me more than it used to."

I lift his leg beneath his knee and gently move his foot out of the car, then follow with the other foot. Sliding my arm under his armpit, I guide him out of the car. He leans against my side, and I brace myself for his weight, but it's as if his bones have turned to styrofoam. They hold his shape, but he's so light and unstable I fear he'd blow away if I wasn't holding him. We walk slowly to the front door, my fear for him growing with each step. I don't let go until we reach the threshold.

Once inside Dad releases my hand. "Thank you."

I stare at his back as he shuffles to the couch. My father has become an old man before my eyes. How have I not seen how drastically he's changed? I don't think he was like this on the way to the doctor, but I've been so absorbed in my own silly life that maybe I didn't notice. "Can I get anything for you?"

"Water would be nice, thank you."

I carry a glass to the living room and set it on the coffee table before sitting next to him. "I'm sorry, I didn't realize how bad it was."

"I haven't wanted to scare you."

"Dad, I don't need protecting. If there's something I can do to make things easier for you, please tell me. There's no reason for you to suffer just so I don't feel bad." My phone buzzes again and I remember the earlier texts that I never checked.

Dad nods at my phone. "Go ahead."

They're all from Cameron.

Cameron: When are you done at the doctor?

Twenty minutes later.

Cameron: Can you come over later?

Another twenty minutes later.

Cameron: Not to be a girl, but hello?

Then just now.

Cameron: So is that a no?

I write back.

Me: Sorry. Just got home.

I look at Dad. "Is it cool if I go to Cam's?"

"Sure. I was beginning to wonder if you two had broken up."

"We did. But now we're back together."

He smiles as if remembering something from long ago. "Ah, high school. Anything you want to talk about?"

I pick at the couch cushion with my fingernail. "Not really. A lot of it has to do with Katie and how she's dealing with everything. He's under a lot of stress and I'm trying to be supportive, but I don't think it's enough."

"I find that hard to believe."

I wink at him. "That's because you have to think I'm perfect." He snorts and I laugh. "Come on, don't burst my bubble now. I thought sending my college applications would earn me some brownie points."

He smiles. "It did."

"So anyway, Cam asked if I can come over tonight to hang out. I'll be home by curfew."

"Tell him hello. And try to be a little more understanding.

They're dealing with a lot."

"I know." I lean over and kiss his cheek before standing. "Thanks Dad."

Me: I'll be over in half in hour.

Chapter 29

The first thing I notice when I turn onto Cameron's street is a van like the one Turner threw me into parked across the street. My breathing comes to a stop for one beat, two, three... then I blink several times to clear my head. This van has the call letters from a local TV station plastered across the side and a satellite dish leans lazily on the roof.

Has Katie seen the van parked out here? If I had that reaction after being in it for less than ten minutes, I can't imagine the reaction she's having.

I park in the driveway behind Old Berta and hustle up the sidewalk before anyone in the van tries to talk to me. Cameron opens the door before I knock.

"I was watching for you. Didn't want the vultures to have a chance to attack."

I look back at the van. A man wearing a baseball cap and bright jacket sits in the driver's seat, while an over-hairsprayed brunette talks on the phone in the passenger seat. "How long have they been here?"

"Since before I got home from school." Cameron shuts the door and I turn my attention to him. His hair and clothes are the same from earlier, but it's like he dropped the mask he wears in public, revealing the sleepless nights and constant stress that have been a part of his life for too long.

"And they're just sitting in the van?"

He shrugs. "I'm guessing they're waiting until my mom or dad gets home. Probably figured they shouldn't try to interview me or Katie."

Being a photographer means I also have a bit of journalist in me, and I can't help but imagine how I would approach this situation. "Maybe they aren't all bad." Cameron raises an eyebrow at me, so I try to explain. "If they were complete slimeballs they wouldn't care about ethics and would just barge up to your front door."

His eyes narrow. "How is stalking us ethical?"

I press my hands to his chest, hoping to diffuse the anger I've clearly lit in him. "I'm not saying—I mean," I take a quick breath. "They're playing by the rules by waiting for your parents. That's all I'm trying to say."

"Whatever." He turns away and walks through the house without inviting me in further. I know I've been here a million times and his house is my house, but the attitude stings. He stops at the end of the hall and holds his hand out in exasperation. "Are you coming?"

Not the romantic greeting I was hoping for, but I guess it will have to do. Now if I can just keep from putting my foot in my mouth the rest of the evening. I follow him into the living room, where Katie is curled up in a chair, her eyes bouncing between the TV and the phone in her lap.

"Hey, Katie," I say as I sit on the end of the couch farthest from her.

She looks at me, then faces Cameron. "Explain to me again why I can't hang out with my friends?"

Cameron sits heavily next to me and rests his hand on my leg. "Mom and Dad told us to stay here until they get home."

"If you hadn't cried to them about that stupid van they wouldn't even know." Katie glances at her phone, then types in a message before glaring at him. "It's not like I want to go play in the front yard. I learned that lesson four years ago."

Cameron sucks in a breath.

"I just want to get out of here."

No wonder Cameron's emotions are all over the place. Katie bounces so quickly between petulant child and jaded victim that all I can do is stare. Yet he keeps trying to reason with her.

"No one is saying you can't go out. Just wait until they're home. Please." There is so much frustration and pleading in the word 'please' that I wonder how long this conversation has been going on.

"Whatever." Her fingers tap out another message, then she crosses her arms and stares pointedly at the TV.

Cameron leans his head against the back of the couch. His lips move like he's talking to himself.

"Serenity prayer?" I whisper.

"Counting to ten." I watch as he mouths eight, nine, and ten, then he lifts his head and laces his fingers through mine. "How'd your appointment go?"

I think of the moment between me and Martinez and warmth flushes my neck. "It was fine. Dad came with me and I told Martinez about flick—" I stop, but Katie isn't paying attention to us.

"You told him? Why?"

I'm on the defensive in a flash. I sit upright. "It's my decision to make. You don't know what it's like not understanding why—"

He touches my face, silencing me. "I didn't mean that the way it sounds. You've worked so hard to keep it a secret I'm just surprised you told him, that's all."

"Amelia knows too."

He smiles. "Now her I expected. I'm surprised you kept it from her so long."

"You and me both."

"So how'd Martinez take it? You're not locked up in the loony bin so I guess that's a good sign."

"He's excited. Wants to start tests next week."

Cameron traces his thumb over my cheek. "And you're okay with that?"

I lean into his caress. "I want to understand this and if becoming his guinea pig saves me from my dad's fate then it's worth it."

266

"Wait, what?"

I mentally scan every conversation we've had about flickering. "You know my dad—" I tilt my head to indicate the word. "Right?"

"What are you talking about?" We both turn to look at Katie, who's staring at us with eyes brighter than I've seen in weeks.

"Nothing." I say quickly.

"It's not nothing. You've got a secret and I want to know."

"No." Cameron says.

"I'll stay home if you tell me."

"You'll stay home because that's what Mom and Dad want."

"Fine, then I'm leaving." She pushes herself out of the chair, slides her phone into her back pocket, and sprints to the front door before we can get to our feet.

"Katie, stop! Please!" Cameron reaches the door just as it slams shut. He yanks it open and I follow him into the front yard.

Katie is already at the news van, waving her hands and yelling at the driver through the open window, who's pointing a camera at her. The brunette from the passenger seat rushes to Katie's side, holding up her hands in an effort to calm Katie. Cameron rushes to Katie and tries to wrangle her flailing arms.

"Katie, come on. Come back inside."

"No!" She yanks free from his grasp and points an arm at the reporter. "They won't leave until they talk to me, so here I am! What do you want to know?"

The reporter stares, mouth open.

Katie sneers at her. "You won't get far with that killer instinct. I can see the headline now. Rape victim flips out as reporter asks nothing."

Cameron's eyes nearly bug out of his head. "Katie, please stop."

But Katie ignores him. She takes a step closer to the reporter, who juts her chin in a small semblance of defiance. "Yes, I know the hearing is coming up. Yes, I think he should rot in jail. But no, I have no intention of ever setting foot in that courtroom."

The reporter locks eyes with the driver, who gives a small nod and pats the top of the camera.

Katie looks at Cameron, her eyes shining with tears. "I'm going out. You can tell Mom and Dad whatever you want." She walks away, each foot set precisely in front of the other, her shoulders tense. When she's a couple houses away, a rusty gray car turns onto the street and stops alongside her. She opens the back door, climbs in, and is gone.

Chapter 30

Back inside, Cameron is completely defeated, and for once I understand. "Is she always like that?"

"That's the first time she's yelled at strangers, but otherwise, yeah."

I start to walk back to the living room, but he heads for the stairs. Not what I was expecting, but okay.

He pauses with his hand on the railing. "Do you mind if we hang out in my room? If we're down here I'm just going to stare at where Katie was sitting."

"Won't your parents freak if I'm up there?"

He shrugs. "They've got bigger things to worry about." He climbs the stairs but I hesitate. Of course I want to be alone with him, but this feels forced. Two minutes ago Katie was screaming at that reporter and now he wants to make out?

I find him in his room, lying on his back on the bed, shoes on the floor. He slides over to make room for me. "Are you sure about this?"

"I just want to be near you. Although we are alone." He winks and my stomach does a little flip. "Come here."

"Aren't you upset about Katie?"

He sighs. "Of course, but I guess I've gotten used to her outbursts. Sitting here worrying isn't going to make her come home any sooner."

I sit on the edge of the bed and kick off my shoes, then twist so I can lie on my back next to him. I feel a little weird being his distraction from Katie, but then his arm slides over my belly and he pulls me closer, making me forget my concern. I turn my head so we're nose to nose and he gives me a quick kiss.

"I'm glad you were here when that happened. If it was just me and Katie I probably would have chased after her and things would have been even worse."

"Not that I did anything to help."

"You helped me." He nuzzles his face into my neck and I

close my eyes. "So what else happened at the doctor?"

"Same stuff as usual, aside from me telling Martinez that I'm a freak of nature."

"Stop. So aside from the tests, what'd he say? How long did it take for him to believe you?"

"He got pretty pissed off at first, which was weird because we usually get along fine. There's a balance to our relationship: I give him a hard time and he eventually makes me answer his questions."

"Your relationship?"

I open my eyes to find Cameron staring at me. "You know what I mean. Relationship, as in how we relate to each other."

"Mm-hmm."

A flash of anger sparks in my chest. "I don't think you're in a position to be questioning relationships."

He props himself up on one elbow. "What's that supposed to mean?"

"You're going to make me say it?"

"What, Sarah?"

I point one finger in the air. "Bingo."

"How many times do I have to tell you that nothing is going

on with her? We're just friends. She understands what I'm—what my family—is going through."

"The same way Martinez is super interested in my brain, but nothing more." I'm still not convinced that nothing happened with Sarah, but if we were broken up then there's not much I can do about it.

Cameron pinches the bridge of his nose with his thumb and forefinger, then exhales slowly before speaking. "Can we put that behind us? She's my friend and I don't see that changing anytime soon."

I want to believe him. Believing him is so much easier than being jealous.

He lowers his head and nuzzles his face against my shoulder. "You're the only one I want to be with."

I dip my head so our mouths touch, a slight pressure that quickly turns insistent, urgent, as Cameron's hands run down my side and across my stomach, just above the top of my jeans. This feels too fast, too rushed. But it's Cameron, the voice in my head whispers. You can trust him.

My fingers lace through his hair, pulling him closer. My lips part, welcoming his tongue as it dances with mine. Heat races through me and I need more of him touching me. As if reading my mind he rolls on top of me, his elbows resting on either side of my head.

"See," he whispers. "I just wanted to be near you."

I laugh softly before wrapping my arms around him. My fingers trace the contours of his spine until I reach the hem of his shirt, then with a quick tug I find bare skin. Our kiss grows deeper and I forget everything but him, this room, this bed. His hand grazes the button on my jeans before sliding beneath my shirt, higher, higher, until he reaches my bra. We instinctively press closer together, setting the room spinning, and before I know it he's yanking his shirt over his head.

His smooth skin nearly sets me on fire. I want to feel more of him against me. With one hand I tug at my shirt, trying to pull it over my head, but the weight of his body holds it in place. He leans on one elbow then slowly, painfully so, lifts my shirt over my chest, then over my head, and drops it to the floor.

I lift my hand to touch his face. His lower lip is swollen from kissing and I run my thumb over it, wondering how something so soft can be so demanding.

He lowers his mouth for another kiss but stops before

touching me. His eyelids are heavy with desire, yet he doesn't move.

"What's wrong?"

"Shit." He reaches for my shirt on the floor, nearly crushing me with his weight. "I think my parents are home."

"Oh crap!" I'm on my feet and dressed in seconds. I reach to smooth my hair and for a moment am surprised to find stubble. I laugh. "You made me forget I'm bald."

Cameron's shirt is over his shoulders but his abdomen is still exposed. "That good, huh?"

I can't help myself. I press my hand against his abs, and he moans softly. "Like you don't know."

The sound of the front door opening kills the moment.

"Go in the bathroom while I run downstairs. They're gonna flip their shit when I tell them about Katie."

When I go downstairs a few minutes later Cameron's parents barely give me a second glance. Cameron nods at the living room and I go in there to wait. Snatches of their conversation drift to me, their voices frightened and panicked.

"Why didn't you stop her?"

"I didn't know what to do."

"What if she doesn't come back?"

Cameron comes in a few minutes later and sits so close to me that our legs are pressed together. He leans over and kisses the spot on my neck just below my ear, sending a shiver through me. "Sorry about that. I thought we had more time."

My nerve endings are still on fire, concentrated wherever we touch. "Should I leave?" From the looks of it they have another evening of sitting around waiting for Katie to come home. How is it that the pattern from when Katie was missing is still their way of life?

"No. They want to watch the news to see if Katie's on there, but they said we can have the living room after that."

I waggle my eyebrows. "No more bedroom?"

He chuckles, a deep sound that comes from his throat. "I wish." His arm wraps around my shoulders, pulling me in for another kiss. I inhale, breathing him in, and twist my fingers into his hair.

"Ahem."

We break apart as if scalded. I burrow my hands between my knees and hunch my shoulders. Cameron's parents stand in the doorway. "Hi, Mr. James. Mrs. James." They each take one of the chairs that flank the couch.

"Hi, Biz," says Mr. James. His hair, dark and thick like Cameron's, sticks out on top like he's been pulling on it.

Mrs. James reaches for the remote and looks at Cameron. "What channel was it?"

Cameron looks at me. "Did you notice the letters on the van?"

You'd think I'd be able to remember four-foot tall letters, but I'm drawing a blank. "I think there was a three?"

Mrs. James changes the channel. "I guess now we wait."

Cameron slips his hand into mine and we wait.

And wait.

The silence is unbearable. Even the commercials do nothing to drown out the tension in the room.

At six o'clock the news jingle plays and we all lean forward. A man with perfect hair and wearing a dark suit smiles grimly into the camera, a skill that seems reserved for people on the news. "Tonight on News at 6, a rollover crash that left a family in a ditch, a three-alarm house fire, and," he cocks his head, "an exclusive reaction from one of the kidnap victims in the upcoming Turner pre-trial hearing."

Mrs. James clamps her hand over her mouth, while

Cameron murmurs a long "ohhhhhhhhh shit" under his breath.

Mr. James looks at us. "How bad was it?"

Cameron waves a hand in the air. "You know, the usual for her. Screaming, hands flailing all over the place, plus a couple snotty comments to the reporter. But I'm pretty sure they'll edit that part out."

We wait through the lead stories and another set of commercials. I don't actually want to see her on TV, but it's like a bad car crash that you can't turn away from—I need to see it. The jingle sounds again and Katie's face fills the screen. From where I'd been standing I didn't realize she was so close to the camera, but you can see every detail: heavy black liner ringing her wide eyes, shaggy hair falling in her face, the sneer that turns her otherwise pretty mouth ugly.

She's pointing at the reporter. "Here I am! What do you want to know?"

The reporter's body is turned so the camera doesn't show her dumbfounded expression.

Katie pauses for a beat—a reaction that only Cameron and I notice—then Katie sneers at her. "I can see the headline now.

Rape victim flips out."

Cameron steps into the frame, eyes full of concern. "Katie, please stop."

Katie moves toward the reporter, who juts her chin, but on camera it plays off like she's listening intently, not holding her ground against an irrational child. "Yes, I know the hearing is coming up. Yes, I think he should rot in jail. But no, I have no intention of ever setting foot in that courtroom."

The scene cuts to the reporter standing in front of the house. "You have it from the victim's mouth: she won't be attending the pre-trial hearing. No words yet from the prosecution on what this could mean for their case, as Ms. James's testimony is crucial for a conviction. Reporting live, this is Jenny Woods."

The anchor launches into the next story and Mrs. James turns off the TV. The remote clatters to the table. "Can they do that? Can they just show up at our house and talk to her like that? She's a minor. There are laws for this, right?" Her eyes fill with tears and she clutches her hands in her lap. She turns to her husband. "I thought she's protected because she's a victim. How can they show her on TV?"

Mr. James sighs heavily and pushes himself out of his chair. "I don't know, but I'm going to find out." He stalks to the kitchen and in moments his deep voice carries into the living room.

"At least they cut out the snotty parts," Cameron says.

"It was worse? Good god." Mrs. James covers her face with her hands. "I don't know what to do for her. Nothing we say seems to get through."

Cameron moves to her side so he's crouching next to her and wraps an arm around her shoulders. "It's okay, Mom. You're doing the best you can. We all are. We just can't give up on her. I know that's what it seems like she wants, but if we didn't give up on her all those years she was gone, we can't give up on her now." She sniffles and Cameron holds her closer.

All those nights that I felt left out because Cameron wouldn't let me come over, this is probably what was going on. Now I get it. The pain from when Katie disappeared is still present in everything they do. Having her back home was only a stopgap—her current suffering is a whole new kind of grief.

I stand. "I should go."

They both look up, tears shining in their eyes, an expression of sadness and anguish mirrored in their faces. Mrs. James dabs the corner of her eye with her sleeve. "No, you kids stay here. If I've learned anything in all this it's that you take your lumps and keep going."

Cameron stands and moves next to me, slipping his hand into mine. "Just another day in the James house. Mom, you sure you don't mind if we watch a movie? We can pick something you like."

She wipes her eyes again, then stands. "No, thank you. But promise me one thing?"

I go rigid, waiting for a reprimand for being caught upstairs earlier.

"Sure, anything."

"Let me know the minute you hear from her."

Chapter 31

I'm snuggled tightly against Cameron's side, but the excitement from earlier has passed. It could be the fact that his parents are in the other room, or the very non-romantic action movie we're watching, but really I have too much on my mind. "I didn't finish telling you about why I told Martinez."

Cameron lowers his head so his forehead is resting on mine. "You said because you want to know why you flicker."

"Yeah, but why I want to know. You know how my dad flickers, too?" He nods against me. "Well, that's why he's always been so sick. It's not epilepsy, it's from years of flickering. He just lets the doctors think what they want to keep them from knowing the truth."

His body tenses.

"He's been getting worse and a couple weeks ago they told him he doesn't have much longer to live."

"What?"

"It could be a couple months, it could be another year, but either way, he's dying." The numbness I feel whenever I think about the world without my dad creeps over me, threatening to swallow me whole.

He twists so he's facing me, his hand gripping my upper arm. "Biz, why didn't you tell me right away?" The panic in his eyes makes me regret telling him. At least tonight.

I lower my eyes. "We weren't exactly talking when I found out. And you have enough to worry about without me adding to it."

He relaxes his grip but doesn't let go of my arm. "Oh."

"Yeah."

"So that's why you decided to talk to Martinez."

"Mm-hmm. Dad is concerned about Martinez's intentions, but I trust him."

"His intentions?" He smirks. "Makes it sound like he's into you or something."

I roll my eyes. "Not you, too."

"I was kidding. Is that what your dad thinks?"

I hold up a hand between us. "Wait. Let me start over before I completely screw this up. I had to convince my dad that telling Martinez was a good idea, so of course he's going to be skeptical, then when we were talking about tests and all that stuff Dad thought Martinez got too friendly with me."

"Oh." He's quiet, and the longer he goes without speaking the more I dread what he'll say next. Why can't a conversation ever go the way I plan? "But he wasn't, right?"

"No! Like I told Dad, he examines my head. Of course he's going to be standing close to me." I study his reaction but his face gives nothing away. "Cam, he's a grown up. You believe me, right?"

The muscles in his face relax and he smiles. "Of course I trust you. You say the wrong thing and totally piss me off sometimes, but I know your heart is in the right place. That's what I love about you."

Hold. The. Phone. "Did you just?"

The corner of his mouth lifts in a shy smile. "I wanted to see if you were listening."

My heart balloons in my chest, stopping my breath. All I can do is stare at him. I guess deep down I assumed he loved me, but it's different to hear it said out loud. "You know I love you, right?"

He traces the side of my face with his fingertips. "I was hoping." He lowers his head until our lips meet. It's the sweetest, most loving kiss I've ever had and I don't want it to end. My whole world is wrapped up in this one boy. With him I can face anything: going away to school, the uncertainty of my health, even my dad's death.

His lips move over my cheek, my eyes, settling on the top of my head. "I do think your dad has a point."

I pull back so I can look in his eyes. "You can trust me."

"It's not you I'm worried about. What if Martinez doesn't have your best interests in mind? This could be huge for someone in his profession. What if he uses you to help his career?"

"He hasn't given me a reason not to trust him, and while it might be too late to save my dad's life, it could help me. If he ends up benefitting from that, I guess that's a price I'm willing to pay." Tears sting my eyes and I press the heel of my hand against them. "How do you put a price on your own life?"

He pulls me into his arms and holds me close. "You can't. Just promise me you'll be careful."

*****

Cameron's words are still ringing in my ears a week later when I'm sitting on the examining table in Martinez's office.

Martinez is pacing back and forth across the office and, despite my uncertainty, his enthusiasm is contagious. "I've already made a list of tests I'd like to start with, but some of them won't be covered by insurance so I may need to apply for a grant. That should get us through the first year, at the very least."

I raise a hand. "Hello?"

He stops near the door and looks at me.

"Grants?"

"Well, yeah. All these tests cost money. If they aren't considered an integral part of your care, the insurance company won't even look at the claims."

"Does this mean you believe me?"

"Not completely. I'd still like to see a recording, if you think you can do it."

I nod. "But that means you have to tell more people." I imagine a dozen gray-haired men in suits sitting around a conference table in an office with floor to ceiling windows overlooking a big city like New York. I don't need them discussing my freakazoid head.

285

"I can be vague in the application. Since your father's doctors seem to think he has epilepsy, I can use that as a basis for the research." He smiles, making him look even younger than he already does. "Who doesn't want a cure for epilepsy?"

"But I don't have epilepsy."

"I know you don't, but I can use your genetic disposition to demonstrate that you might."

"Because of my dad."

"Yes."

"But we didn't say..." I trail off. Arguing that my dad doesn't—well, didn't—flicker is stupid.

"Not in so many words but it wasn't hard to put two and two together." He taps the side of his head. "I am a brain surgeon, after all."

Twenty different reactions fight to burst from my mouth, but I hold them back. It's one thing for me to decide to tell my secret, but it doesn't feel right to talk about Dad when he's not here.

"I just want to help you." He moves to the edge of the examining table and grabs my hand, holding it between his. "You can trust me."

I look down at our hands. Mine seem tiny compared to his and I feel safe here, protected.

But Dad's voice saying that this is inappropriate clears Martinez's excitement from my head. It's like his touch casts a weird spell over me that throws logic out the window. I pull my hand away and tuck it under my leg.

Martinez is still waiting for a response.

I tilt my head. "I don't suppose you'd consider signing a confidentiality agreement."

His head jerks back as if I've slapped him, but instead of pulling away he steps closer. "Biz, I want to find out why this happens to you and save your life. That's all. You can trust me."

He looks into my eyes and despite Cameron's and Dad's warning shouting inside my head, butterflies fill my stomach. I want to trust him. His pleading eyes make it difficult not to agree to whatever he wants.

"I know that, at least I think I do, but I can't go home and tell my dad 'Hey, Martinez is planning to tell a ton of people about the secret you've guarded your entire life.' That won't go over real well."

A soft laugh escapes him. "That's not how a grant works, but I understand your concern. And please, call me Rick."

Now the warning bells are really clanging. I try to run my

hand through my hair, an old habit that's continued even though I have nothing to run it through, but I end up scratching the back of my neck, which is not only not subtle, it's super sexy. Not that I'm trying to be sexy. Good god, are they pumping drugs into the office?

Martinez—I am not calling him Rick, that's just weird— turns away to grab his notepad from the counter. "Talk to your dad about the grant, and tell him to call me with any concerns. In the meantime, there's something I'd like to ask you that only requires permission from you." His brown eyes come alive and once again I find myself eager to hear whatever comes from his lips.

"What's that?"

He takes a deep breath and reads something on his notepad before looking into my eyes. "I'd like to be the one to record you when you flicker."

Chapter 32

"I don't like the idea of you being alone in a car with him," Dad says.

We're sitting at the kitchen island, a plate of freshly baked chocolate chip cookies between us. Half a plate, actually, because sometimes a girl needs a little chocolate to help her make life-altering decisions.

I don't either, but I'm not going to tell him that. Part of me is drawn to Martinez in a way that makes me nervous. Maybe it's the fact that unlike Cameron, he doesn't accuse me of being unsupportive. He makes me feel like what I say and how I'm doing are important. "Technically, I've already ridden in a vehicle with him."

Dad tilts his head.

"The last time an ambulance had to come get you." I tap my chin. "When you kicked me in the face."

"I still feel bad about that."

I reach for his hand. "I was due for another round of child abuse." That gets a smile out of him, but it doesn't last. "True, it would be different than catching a ride home from him in an ambulance, but it's nothing I can't handle."

"Biz, if you're not one-hundred percent comfortable with this, you shouldn't do it."

"It's not that I'm uncomfortable, it's just..." I trail off. Big mistake.

Dad leans forward, eyes narrowed. "Did something happen?"

"Not really, he's just super excited and it feels like it's moving really fast." I choose not to mention the 'Rick' thing. "I realize Martinez is a doctor and of course he wants to get all sciencey and solve the puzzle that is my brain, but I guess I was expecting Cameron and Amelia's reactions. A lot of shock, a little awe, then acceptance."

"Do you regret telling him?"

"I've had second thoughts since the moment we told him,

but I don't think I regret it. I really do want to find out why this happens to me and he's my best chance. I knew there was the risk that he'd tell people, but I figured that was years down the road." I grab another cookie and force down a bite, but the chocolate does nothing to calm my thoughts. "Plus, deep down I'm still hanging on to the hope that it might not be too late for you, that Martinez might figure out a way to save your life."

He rubs his hand over his face. "Biz, it's too late for me. I wish it wasn't, but there's nothing Martinez or anyone else can do."

I blink back tears. "How can you know that?"

"My body is tired. I don't have much fight left. So now we need to concentrate on saving you."

"What would happen if everyone found out?"

Dad stares at the plate for several moments before meeting my eyes. "That's a fear I've lived with my entire life. It's too late to unring that bell, so all we can do now is hope that he solves your brain before the world finds out." He smiles at the words I used earlier, but I'm freaking out over the last thing he said.

The world?

My phone buzzes in my pocket, momentarily stopping my panic.

Cameron: Katie's missing. I need your help.

I feel worn out, defeated, and I don't know if I have the energy to help right now. But I have to. "I need to go to Cam's. Katie's missing again."

"Missing? Again?"

I shake my head. "Sorry, not like that. She keeps sneaking out and Cam doesn't want his parents to freak out so he tries to find her before they know she's gone."

Me: Be there soon.

"He shouldn't have to bear that responsibility on his own."

"Tell me about it. I feel responsible, too, since I'm the one who brought her back."

"Biz, you saved her from hell. Any responsibility you have for her stopped there." I'm already out of my chair but he reaches for my arm. "You didn't cause this."

I try to smile but my mouth refuses to cooperate. I may not be directly responsible for what Katie's been through, but I feel like I set her on this path. All I want is for the sweet little girl who vanished from her yard to return, but that's never going to happen. "Thanks, Dad. But I need to help her."

His hand drops to his side and he slumps back in his chair.

It's moments like these when I notice how much he's aged in the past year.

Will that happen to me, too?

I hate to leave, but the need to help Katie, to be there for Cameron, pushes me forward. I give Dad a peck on the cheek. "I have to go. Don't plan on me for dinner." I'm opening the front door when I hear him call after me.

"Please be safe."

Cameron's waiting by Old Berta when I arrive at his house. I park beneath a streetlight across the street and approach him, hands stuffed in my pockets. "Are we going somewhere?"

He pulls me against him and I press my cheek to his chest. I'd be okay with doing this all night, but that's not why I'm here. "I thought maybe we could drive around and try to find that gray car that picked her up the other day. Nate's not old enough to drive, but he has friends who are."

I pull my head back so I can look at him. "You're serious?"

"I don't know what else to do." He opens the passenger door for me and I get in.

"I assume you've called her friends."

He starts the car and we ease onto the street. "The ones I

know about. She doesn't share much with me." The hurt in his voice and the desperation on his face make me check my attitude. Right now he needs me to support him, not second-guess him.

We weave through the neighborhoods closest to Cameron's house before heading to the other side of town. A quiet part of me wishes he'd ask how I'm doing. He acts like I'm not supportive, but the same could be said of him. Anytime he's asked for help I've been there. We pass through the Strand and I press my forehead against the window. The tall trees don't pose a threat at night so I can admire them without fear.

Cameron notices me looking up at them. "Do you think you can flicker with moonlight?"

"I don't know." The faint light reaching through the branches seems too weak to have any effect on me. "I've never really thought about it." The moonlight may not be bright enough to make me flicker, but it does cause a rippling effect on Cameron's hand that grips the steering wheel. My heart feels too full for this boy. I reach for his other hand, the one resting on the gear shift. "We'll find her."

We turn into a neighborhood on the way to the boat ramp, but it's getting too dark to distinguish one car from the next. Cameron slams his arm against the door. "This is stupid. We're never going to find it."

"Try calling her again."

He pulls the car to the side of the road and hits redial. I hold my breath as we wait for an answer, but it never comes. He ends the call and rests his forehead on the steering wheel. "I don't know what else to do."

I take a breath and suggest the one person I don't want to. "Have you tried Sarah? Maybe she's with Maddy."

"I texted her earlier but she said she wasn't there. I'll try her again." He scrolls through his contacts to find her number and I feel a small prick of satisfaction that she's not in his speed dial list. "Hey Sarah, it's Cam. I still haven't heard from Katie." He drums him fingers on the steering wheel. "Okay, thanks." He hangs up and looks at me. "She hasn't heard from her. Maddy's been in her room since school."

"So what now?"

"I don't know." He puts his head in his hands and I reach for him, pulling him close.

I hold him awkwardly, leaning across the center console with my arms wrapped around him, wishing there was some way I could fix this.

After a few minutes we break apart and he puts the car in drive. "We should go home."

Does that mean both of us to his home or to our separate houses? I want to be there for him, but I don't want to be in the way. Based on his clenched jaw and narrowed eyes, this is not the time for neurotic girlfriend questions. When we pull into his driveway I'm still no closer to knowing what he wants. I get out of the car and slowly close the door. "Do you want me to stay?"

He pauses in the middle of the driveway. He looks lost, as if he's surprised to find himself at home. "Can you?"

I hurry to his side and slip an arm around his waist. "Of course. I'll stay as long as you want."

That turns out to be longer than I expected. I wake up on the couch in his living room as the first hints of dawn crawl across the ceiling. Cameron's arms hold me against his chest, our legs intertwined. His parents must have gone to bed shortly after they went upstairs.

His phone buzzes. That must be what woke me.

"Cam." I press my palm to his chest. "Cam," I whisper louder. "Your phone."

His eyes open a crack and he smiles softly at me. "Good morning," he whispers, before brushing his lips against mine.

This is most definitely how I want to wake up every morning, but this will have to wait. "Check your phone," I mumble against his lips.

"Hmm? Oh." He rolls over me to reach his phone, then resumes his sleep position. With one hand he checks his texts. "It's Sarah. She says to call right away." All traces of sleep vanish as he makes the call.

I prop myself on my elbow to give him room. "Please let her be okay. Please let her be okay." I don't realize I'm talking out loud until Cameron gives me a pleading look.

"Sarah, what's going on?"

Her garbled voice reaches me through the phone. I can't make out her words, but there's no need. The blood drains from Cameron's face and he drops the phone.

I grab the phone and press it to my ear but all I hear is crying. "Cameron, what happened?"

His mouth falls open but nothing comes out.

I try the phone. "Sarah?"

She sniffles. "It's Katie." Her voice cracks, and a new wave of sobs fills my ears as tears slide down Cameron's face. Sarah clears her throat. "She's dead."

Chapter 33

This can't be right.

Katie is not dead.

Sarah is wrong.

The pressure in my chest that seems constant these days is almost too much to bear, but I push it down. Right now I need to help Cameron, and falling apart will only complicate whatever the hell is going on.

Cameron pushes himself off the couch. "I have to tell my parents."

"Wait! Are you sure? This can't be real. She can't be—"

He touches the top of my head, letting his hand brush across my cheek, then hang limply at his side. "Sarah found her in the bathroom at her house."

I sit, stunned, as he walks away and climbs the stairs. I hear a knock, a creak as a door opens, then moments later, a scream.

I jump up from the couch. I shouldn't be here for this. They need to be alone. I move toward the front door but stop in the hallway. I can't just leave without saying anything. And Cameron needs me.

Shit.

I pace the hallway, debating which is worse: to be standing here when his parents come down or for Cameron to think I've abandoned him right when he needs me the most.

I decide to wait. Being uncomfortable in front of his parents, or even having them ask me to leave, is nothing compared to losing Cameron. And if he thinks for two seconds that I don't care, I might not be able to repair that damage.

Shouts drifts down the stairs and I freeze.

Coffee. I should make coffee. I fumble around the cupboard near the coffeemaker for filters, shove one in the top of the machine, then dump fresh grounds inside, followed by a pot of water. In moments the machine whirs to life, filling the kitchen with the heady aroma of brewed coffee. I'm pulling mugs from another cupboard when Cameron enters the kitchen.

I motion to the coffeemaker. "I needed to do something." As soon as I say those words, realization hits me and I know what I need to do.

"Thank you." His voice is monotonous, flat. A light seems to have gone out in his eyes as he watches me from across the room. He just stands there like he doesn't know what to do. "My dad talked to Sarah's parents. Katie—" he chokes back a sob, holding his fist to the base of his throat and swallowing hard. "Katie took a bottle of sleeping pills from Sarah's mom and—" he stops again.

I inch toward him. I've never seen him this... off balance. He reminds me of a wild animal that will spook with one wrong move. I stop in front of him but don't make contact.

"They found her on the bathroom floor. The paramedics are there now."

I rest a hand on his arm. "I'm going back."

His vacant eyes slowly focus on my face, then he shakes his head once, a quick movement that brings a hint of color to his cheeks. "Are you sure? How will you—" he looks down. "How will you stop her?"

"I have no idea." Even if I flicker and am able to get to her in time, I've never dealt with someone who wants to kill herself.

He grabs me by the shoulders and squeezes a little too hard. I flinch, but he doesn't seem to notice. "Biz, you have to save her. I tried but—" Another sob wracks his chest and he slides his hands over my back, pulling me roughly to his chest. "She can't be gone, she can't. Not after we just got her back."

I let him hold me, but the emotional and physical weight on my chest leaves me struggling for breath. We should have been able to stop her. Why didn't I do more, especially after the scene in my bathroom? Everyone knew she was messed up but instead of confronting her, we just let her do whatever she wanted.

Cameron's arms tighten around me and I reach up to stroke his hair. I'll be able to breathe in a minute. This can't last forever. His tears dampen my neck, soaking into my shirt. "I should have seen this coming."

But we did. At my party. I assumed Cameron told his parents about it, but now isn't the time to bring that up. "I know." My face is pressed into his shirt so my voice is muffled. I try to pull away but he's holding me too tightly. "Cam." I wedge my hand between our bodies and push, but he doesn't react. A tremor of fear whispers through me. "Cam!" I shout, and he finally looks at me. "You're hurting me."

His jumps back like he's been scalded and I rub my hand against my chest. He seems to go in and out of focus, like he knows I'm here but isn't quite sure what's going on.

"I'll go back to try to stop her, but before I do we need to figure out what I'm supposed to say. I've never done anything like this before."

"Let's go now. The sun is almost up." He grabs his car keys off the counter, then grips my arm and pulls me toward the front door.

I plant my feet, pulling back so I'm bent over. "Cam, stop!"

He turns on me and for a split second I'm afraid of him. His eyes are glazed over and his entire body is wound tight like a string ready to snap. His fists flex once, twice, before relaxing.

"I'm not going right this second."

"Why?"

"I need to go home. My parents have no idea where I am." And I need half an hour to look up suicide prevention and become a clinical psychologist who specializes in post-traumatic stress. "A couple hours isn't going to change anything. I'll still be back in plenty of time to stop her."

The adrenaline that's been pushing him since Sarah called seems to leave him in one big whoosh. He crumples to the floor and I rush to his side, wrapping an arm around his neck and brushing his hair off his forehead with the other hand.

He looks in my eyes and the desperation nearly crushes me. "The sooner you go back, the sooner this stops. I can't—I don't want my parents to suffer any longer than they have to."

"I promise I'll do it. I just need an hour or two."

"Can I drive you?"

"I don't think that's a good idea. You need to stay with your parents." I don't mention the fact that being behind the wheel may not be the best idea considering he can't even focus on me.

"Do you want someone to drive you?"

Martinez and the promise I made him immediately come to mind, but just as quickly, I dismiss it. This won't be a regular flicker. This is a desperate attempt to save Katie's life. Martinez can wait.

"I'll figure it out." I place my hands on either side of his head and kiss him firmly. "Go be with your parents. I'll text you when I'm ready to go."

"Thank you."

As soon as I'm in the car I call Amelia.

"This better be good." Her voice is heavy with sleep.

"Can you come over right now?"

"You woke me up."

"I know. I'm sorry. This is urgent."

"Life and death?"

A lump catches in my throat. "Yes."

"Be right there."

Chapter 34

Mom and Dad are sitting at the kitchen island when I get home. Mom takes a sip of her coffee. "I can't wait to hear this."

I sit in the chair next to Dad and put my head in my hands. "It's worse." I give them the highlights—searching for Katie, falling asleep at Cameron's, then the panicked call from Sarah.

Dad rests his hand on my leg. We make eye contact and he gives me a nod.

I nod back.

"Amelia's on her way over. I'll be in my room." The weight of everything that's happened catches up to me as I climb the stairs. The lump that's been lodged in my throat hardens and I stop to catch my breath as tears stream down my face. I know in a couple hours I'll go back and try to change things, but right now Katie is dead.

A hand on my back startles me. I turn to find Mom standing over me, tears in her eyes. I fall into her arms and let her rock me like she did when I was a little kid. "I can't believe she's gone. We tried so hard to save her but it wasn't enough."

She rubs her hand in small circles on my back. I wish I could return to the days when her touch could soothe any hurt, but this is too big.

When I feel I can't cry anymore, I straighten and rub my eyes. "Thanks."

The corners of her mouth turn down, but it's a look of concern, a look filled with love. "You're allowed to feel pain, too. I know you've got this idea that you have to fix everything for everyone, but you're not a superhero. You're just a teenage girl. There's only so much you can do."

"I know."

She touches my chin, lifting my head so I'm looking in her eyes. "Do you?"

A knock at the door saves me from answering. "That must be Amelia." I disentangle myself from her embrace and go downstairs to open the door for Amelia. As soon as I see her I burst into tears again.

Her face goes white. "When you said life or death I thought you were being dramatic."

I shake my head and she follows me inside. "We'll be in my room."

Amelia looks from me to my parents then back to me. "Good morning, Clements." Once in my room she tosses her bag on the floor and sits on the bed. "Okay, what the hell is going on?"

I sink onto the floor near her feet. "Katie killed herself."

Her hand flies over her mouth. It's one of the few times I've ever seen her speechless.

I answer the questions I know are flying through her head, finishing with, "Cam wants me to flicker to stop her."

"You have to!"

"I know, but it's bigger than that. The only time I've ever gone back to do something important I screwed it up so bad I ended up getting kidnapped."

"But you still saved Katie and those other girls. Turner's in jail because of you."

"I know, but—" I pick at a piece of carpet, unable to look at her as I voice my deepest fear. "What if I can't stop her? What if I go back and she still kills herself?" Mom's words come back to me. "I'm not a superhero."

Amelia slides off the bed so she's practically sitting in my lap. "What time do you need to go?"

I shrug. "A couple hours."

"Okay. So we've got a couple hours to come up with a plan. Let's hit up the suicide prevention websites and go from there."

I smile for the first time in what feels like days.

She pokes my cheek. "Is that a yes?"

"Yes."

I type "suicide prevention" in the search bar and a list of sites flood the screen. I click the first one and Amelia points at a tab labeled "Get Help for Someone Else." My breath catches, stuck behind a lump in my throat. What made me think I can actually stop Katie?

Amelia rests her head against my shoulder. "We can probably skip the warning signs." My finger hovers over the trackpad while I scan the list.

> Talking about feeling hopeless or having no reason to live.

Talking about feeling trapped or in unbearable pain.

Talking about being a burden to others.

Increasing the use of alcohol or drugs.

Acting anxious or agitated; behaving recklessly.

Sleeping too little or too much.

Withdrawing or isolating themselves.

Showing rage or talking about seeking revenge.

Displaying extreme mood swings.

I blink several times to clear my eyes. I mentally ticked off three or four, but only the first half of the list. And everyone feels that way sometimes.

Amelia nudges me. "Sounds like half the kids at school. What teenagers don't have mood swings?" I navigate to a list written by survivors of suicide and Amelia reads aloud. "Encourage your friend to have goals and dreams, to think beyond what's going on right now. Hopelessness and aloneness can be dealt with."

My eyes focus on the next line: Don't be afraid to talk about suicide. Don't be afraid that talking will make it happen.

She faces me. "How are you going to do this?"

I shake my head. "I don't know. I don't think I can make it

worse, but what am I supposed to do? Bust in her room and spout off that she should stop dwelling on what Turner did to her and instead think about what she wants to be when she grows up?"

"Shoving your cell phone at her and calling the suicide lifeline probably won't go over real well."

We're still huddled over my computer when there's a soft knock at the door. Dad opens it a crack. "Can I come in?"

"Please."

Amelia gives me a sideways look.

"It's okay. He knows."

Dad stands behind us and looks at the website on the screen. "I figured you were going back. What's your plan?"

I sigh, a long, drawn-out exhale that seems to empty me of more than just my breath. "I don't know how I'm going to do this." I look up at him. "Katie doesn't—didn't—listen to me when I was trying to help her with stupid everyday crap."

"I'm no expert, but I'd start with telling her how much everyone loves her and needs her in their lives." Dad touches my shoulder. "I couldn't imagine my life without you. Tell her that."

Amelia leans forward. "What if you point out that if she kills herself, Turner wins?"

"It's worth a shot. I don't think she'll listen to any clichés about how special she is or how she'll get past this. Right now she's desperate. If I can make her feel something else, even if it's anger, that might make her change her mind."

"When are you going?" Dad asks.

"Soon."

He looks at Amelia. "Are you driving?"

She looks back and forth between us. "Driving?"

"I could go by myself, but I'd like it if you could drive me." As far as I can tell Amelia has forgiven me for not telling her about flickering, but I really want her to know that I trust her.

"Sure, of course. Just point me in the right direction."

Dad kisses me on the top of the head. "Good luck. I'm proud of you."

The lump in my throat comes back and a fresh wave of tears spill over my lashes. I stand so I can give him a hug, and the frailty of his body makes me cry even harder. I can try to stop Katie from dying, but nothing I do will save him from that same fate.

He presses a hand to the back of my head, holding me. "This isn't the time to think about me. Focus on Katie."

I nod, not sure how to turn off those thoughts. "I'll try."

Amelia and I spend the next hour plotting every possible scenario. When she envisions me sword-fighting with Katie to keep her from the bottle of pills, I hold up my hands. "Enough. Let's go."

Mom and Dad are mysteriously absent as we pass through the kitchen. Once in Amelia's car I point her toward the Strand.

"That's where you flicker?"

"It's not the only place, but the trees are so tall there that the light does its thing pretty much any time of day."

"Huh."

"Yeah. It sucks when I end up here when I'm not planning to go back."

She smirks. "I bet."

"Listen, there's something else I need you to do." I turn on my phone and open the video app.

She glances at the phone. "A little pre-flickering video confession?"

A smile twitches my mouth. "I need you to record me. Then when I say so, throw the phone in my lap."

"What's this for?"

313

"Martinez." This feels inappropriate—disrespectful, even—but if I want to convince him flickering is real, I need to record myself. I press the red button and check that the volume is on, then hand Amelia the phone.

She points it at my head and I nod.

We round a bend and the Strand comes into sight.

"Do I need to go a certain speed? Will the bomb explode if I drop below fifty?"

I smack her leg. "No, just drive like you are." I bite my lip. I'm not sure if I'm ready.

"You're really brave for doing this."

"I could never live with myself if I didn't."

"I know, but not everyone would be willing to try."

Try. Because I might not succeed. Katie might still kill herself.

We're in the trees now. The light dances over the dashboard, washing over me, engulfing us. Amelia glances at me from the corner of her eye, her left hand locked on the steering wheel.

I wait, and wait, and wait, and—

There! Finally! The tingling zips through my fingers and toes and I lean my head back, willing it to overcome me. But the heaviness never comes. The tingling slows. And we're leaving the Strand.

We round the bend and Amelia slows the car to a crawl before stopping on the side of the road. "Did it work?"

I sit forward, staring at my hands, turning them over and back again. "No, it didn't."

"Is that normal?"

"What about this is normal?"

"Biz, you've never been normal."

I snort. "Thanks."

"What went wrong?"

"I have no idea. That's never happened before." Did I look away from the light? Is the sun not bright enough? Or what if because I want this so badly, it just won't work?

"Let's try again." Amelia waits for a car to pass, then flips the car around so we're driving back into the Strand. "Pay attention this time."

I laugh again. "I'll try."

In moments the tingling is back, this time followed by the glorious heaviness that pushes me deep into the seat. "It's... working..." I gasp. She grabs my hand but I shake her off. I've never touched anyone while I flickered and I don't want to find out what happens now. The heaviness passes and I'm floating to the ceiling. "The... phone..." It lands in my lap.

"Good luck—"

I jerk awake in Trig class. Of course.

Chapter 35

What's slower than a crawl, because that's how today is passing. I've opened the video of me flickering a couple times, but I haven't gotten past the first few seconds when Amelia jokes about how fast she has to drive. All that can wait. I'm too focused on Katie.

When I finally get to Cameron's I drag him to his room. If I could pay someone else to tell him about Katie, I would. Once he's sitting, I catch him up on the past day. When I tell him about Sarah's call he crumples in a heap on the bed, face tucked against his arm, shoulders shaking. He lifts his head, and his tear-streaked face nearly loosens the hold I have on my own emotions. "I know she's having a hard time, but I didn't know it was this bad."

"It is."

"She really killed herself?"

I nod. I don't know if I have the strength to say any more.

He seems to digest this, rolling the idea around in his head, before sitting up. "And you came back to stop her?"

I nod again.

He wipes his face, then rises to his feet. "Then let's go get her."

"That's why I'm here. But we can't just barge into Sarahs' and drag her home. That will only postpone what happens." I touch my palm to his cheek. "We have to make her want to live."

"She knows that we love her and that we'll do anything to help her."

"That's not enough. Right now she can't see past what's happened to her. All she wants is to make the pain go away. She needs to feel hope, anger, anything, if we're going to change her mind."

He tilts his head. "When did you become a psychiatrist?"

"This morning, right before I flickered."

"Okay, so how do we do this?" He paces the small room, reaching each wall in only a handful of steps.

"We go to Sarah's and talk to Katie."

"What if she won't listen?"

A shudder passes through me. "She has to."

"Do you think she's already there?"

"Call Sarah and make her go into Maddy's room. Don't let her just knock on the door." I settle on the edge of the bed while he places the call.

"Hey, it's me. Is Katie there?"

Me? He's 'me' to her?

"Can you check Maddy's room? You know I wouldn't ask if it wasn't important."

I bite my lip. Negative thoughts are not helping.

He moves the phone away from his mouth. "Maddy says she's not there."

"Did she go inside?"

"Sarah, can you please check her room?"

I suppress my concern over Sarah. Saving Katie is our number one priority and we need all the help we can get.

"Okay, thanks. We'll be right over." He closes his phone and comes to a stop in front of me. "She's there."

I stand. "Let's go."

My nerves have the better of me by the time we pull into Sarah's driveway.

Sarah's waiting at the door and opens it as we get out of the car. She approaches Cameron, giving me nothing more than a sidelong glance. "Are you going to tell me what this is about?"

Cameron looks at me, then back at Sarah, stalling. We spent so much time planning what to say to Katie that we never thought about what to tell Sarah.

I step forward. "We're worried she might try to hurt herself. Cam found something that looked like a suicide note in her room."

Lame, but it might work.

Sarah looks surprised. "You went in her room? You never go in her room. Respect her space and all that."

My blood pressure spikes. Why does Sarah know this about him?

Cameron runs his fingers though his hair. Sarah's eyes follow his every movement. "Yeah, well, I freaked when she didn't come home from school or answer her phone. I thought there might be something in her room that'd give me an idea where she was."

I move next to Cameron and loop my arm through his. "We just want to talk to her. To make sure she's okay."

Sarah clenches her jaw and nods. "Sure, come on in."

Cameron heads for the stairs and for the millionth time in the past five minutes I wonder how well they actually know each other. "Biz, do you mind waiting down here? I want to talk to her first."

"Sure?" It comes out as a question, and he stops to look at me. "You okay?"

I shoo him up the stairs. "Yes, go. I'll be down here feeling wildly out of place."

Sarah snorts and I smile at her. Okay, maybe she's not all bad.

Ten minutes later we're sitting at the kitchen table, still waiting for Cameron to announce he's saved Katie. Whatever moment Sarah and I had ended the second he left the room and was replaced with the loudest silence I've ever experienced. My mother's voice keeps telling me to make small talk, to quit being so rude, but anything I might ask seems stupid compared to why we're here.

I'm lost in memories of Katie before she was kidnapped— playing in the park with a bright purple bouncy ball, her squeals of laughter startling the birds resting in the trees high above us—when a door slams upstairs. Cameron appears in the kitchen a moment later. I stand. "Well?"

He shakes his head. "She doesn't want to listen to me. I think I understand why she feels so desperate but I don't know how to get through to her." He touches my face, caressing my cheek with his thumb. "It's up to you."

Out of the corner of my eye I see Sarah turn away. I close my eyes and take a deep breath. When I open them I see nothing but Cameron's dark pleading eyes.

"Which room is Maddy's?"

Chapter 36

I knock on the door at the end of the hall, and after a moment Maddy shouts, "What?"

"It's Biz. Can I talk to Katie?"

"She's not here."

I lean my forehead against the door. "Please?"

The door opens so quickly I stumble forward, falling into Maddy, who jumps backward without ever taking her hand off her hip. "You just had to say the magic word."

Was I ever this obnoxious? "Thanks."

Katie's curled up in a ball on the bed, her back pressed into the corner where the two walls meet. "What is this, good cop, bad cop? I told Cam, I'm not leaving with you guys."

I grab a pink plastic chair from near Maddy's desk and move it closer to the bed. I tuck one leg beneath me and sit. "I'm not here to ask you to leave."

"Well, if you're here to hang out, your hands are way too empty." She winks at Maddy, who reaches inside her closet and retrieves a bottle of vodka. She hands it to Katie, who twists off the cap and takes a quick drink. Her nose wrinkles, but just for a second, then the sneer is back in place. She tilts the bottle toward me but I hold up a hand.

"I'm good."

"Suit yourself." She takes another pull before leaning forward to hand the bottle to Maddy, who takes several sips. I never really paid much attention to Maddy, but the desperation doesn't cling to her as ferociously as it does to Katie. They're dressed the same and seem to have the same attitude, but with Maddy it feels forced, like she's trying to keep up with Katie. Maybe she knows what Katie's planning.

"Katie, your family is worried about you. I'm worried about you. This," I wave my hand at the bottle, "isn't the way to handle things.

She plants her hands on either side of her. Her voice comes

324

out a growl. "Who are you to tell me how to handle things? Just because you're dating my brother doesn't mean you're my friend."

"That's not true. I've loved you like a sister for practically your whole life. Have you forgotten all the time we used to spend together, or have you just blocked it out? Because you're more to me than just someone's little sister."

The harshness around her eyes softens, but just for a moment. "Anything you have to say to me is pointless."

"What if I tell you that I'm the reason you were rescued."

"Rescued? You mean brought from one hell to another? Sure, I'm not being raped anymore but the shit inside my head doesn't go away just because I'm back in my old room. I'll never be able to undo what he did, and nothing you or my family says or does is going to change that."

Maddy whimpers softly, and I feel myself pulled into a dynamic that seems long established.

I look at Maddy. "Did she protect you from him?"

Maddy's mouth falls open but instead of answering, she looks at Katie.

"Don't answer her!"

She doesn't have to. Bits and pieces of what these girls went through, of what they did to survive, fall into place around me. Katie's right. I have no business being here. But Cameron is counting on me to get through to her.

Katie glares at me. "You've known me for a long time, but Maddy is the only one who understands me, who truly gets what I lived through. This is the only place where I don't feel like I'm constantly being watched, like people are wondering what exactly he did to me and if I'm finally going to snap. Even you. Right now I can see the wheels turning, waiting, watching. Always wondering when I'm going to go off the deep end."

I feel like she punched me in the gut. It takes a second to catch my breath, and another before I can speak. "I'm not asking you to leave, I'm just asking you not to do anything stupid. If you do," I pause to take another breath, "he wins."

She seems to consider this and for a moment I think I might have broken through. Her face crumples and the young girl I knew so many years ago reappears. "Don't you get it? He's already won." Tears threaten to spill but she no longer seems to care.

"No, Katie, that's not true." I'm on my knees at the edge of the bed, the closest I dare get to her. My fingers knead the

326

blanket as I scramble to keep her talking.

"But he has. Look at me. I'm broken." She looks down at herself and seems to recoil at what she sees. "Whatever was good in me is gone."

Shit. This isn't going the way I planned. She's supposed to get angry, not get more distraught. "I don't believe that. That's him talking. And you can't let him win."

She wipes her eyes with the edge of the blanket, then wraps it tightly over her shoulders, cocooning herself from the world. Her head shakes slowly from side to side.

"Please, Katie," I want to hug her but settle for resting my hand on her leg. "Think of everyone who loves you. I know it doesn't feel like it right now, but you will get past this."

Her lips form a tight line and her eyebrows narrow.

I pushed it too far.

"Leave. Me. Alone." She kicks my hand away and points at the door.

I stand but stay next to the bed. "I'm sorry. Look, I don't know what you went through and I would never pretend to understand, but I was here all those years you were gone and I saw what it did to your parents. To Cameron. You think you're alone in this, but you're not."

Katie rises on her knees and thrusts her entire arm at the door. "Get out!" Her shout hurts more than just my ears and I flinch, defeated.

On my way to the door I stop in front of Maddy, who had pressed herself flat against the wall. Another technique she learned to protect herself from Turner? "Please don't let her do anything stupid."

Her wide eyes stare back at me but she neither nods nor shakes her head.

Great.

Back downstairs I find Cameron in the chair I'd been sitting in. Sarah's chair is ever-so-slightly closer than it was when we were waiting for Cameron. "That was a bust."

Sarah rolls her eyes. "Did you really think you could waltz in here and magically fix her? That girl has serious problems." Cameron straightens and she seems to realize what she said. "I mean, they both do, after everything they experienced." She reaches for Cameron's arm but he pulls away. "Cam, you know what I mean."

His jaw flexes. "Are there any sleeping pills in the house?"

Sarah's head jerks at his sudden change of topic, but he's on the right track. If we can't get Katie to want to live, we have to take away her weapon.

"Um, my mom might have some, why?"

"Can you get them?" I ask.

She scowls at me. "Sorry, I'm not into that sort of thing. Maybe you like to—"

Cameron slaps his hand on the counter, silencing her. "We're afraid Katie might try to..." He doesn't finish, but based on the way Sarah's mouth falls open, she's finally figured out why we want them.

"I'll go check." She takes the stairs two at a time, leaving us alone in the kitchen.

I reach for his hand. "I really thought I was getting through to her. She dropped the attitude and was actually talking, but I screwed up and said the garbage on that website and she shut down again."

Cameron squeezes my hand. "Thank you for trying. If we can find those pills and—" he shakes his head.

"What?"

"Do you think we should stay here?"

I would like nothing less than spending the night here, but if it helps Katie, I'd fly to the moon. "Probably. But I'm not fighting over you all night."

He looks surprised. "What are you talking about?"

Sarah returns to the kitchen empty-handed. "I couldn't find them."

Cameron stands. "I'm going to try again." He hustles up the stairs without another word, leaving me and Sarah staring at each other. I return to my chair while she leans against the counter, as far away from me as possible without leaving the room.

A muffled shout carries down the stairs. Moments later a door opens and closes, then Cameron comes down the stairs, an amber-colored bottle in his hand. "I found these in her backpack." He sets them on the counter.

I reach for them, but Sarah grabs them before I can see the label.

"They're my dad's."

Cameron looks over her shoulder. "Are they sleeping pills?"

She shakes her head. "Vicodin. Pain pills."

He looks at me. "Do you think they're the right ones?"

They were sleeping pills before, not pain pills, but I can't say that in front of Sarah. "I don't know."

"What are you talking about?"

Cameron avoids her question. "Sarah, do you think your parents would let us stay over?"

Her pretty mouth purses into an even prettier pout that I'd have to bet she spends hours practicing. "Both of you?"

"Yeah," we both say.

Sarah gets permission from her parents under the guise that we're worried about Katie and want to be near her. They've been through so much with Maddy that they've long stopped questioning these things. If it makes the girls happy, they do it.

After a quick call to Dad to tell him where I am, we settle in for the night—Sarah in her room, me on the couch, and Cameron on the floor next to me—but I can't sleep. This has to be the most bizarre situation I've been in yet.

Chapter 37

I wake to the gentle sounds of Cameron snoring. I never knew he snored, but then again before last night, well, both last nights, I've never slept next to him. I swing my arm over the side of the couch and tap his shoulder. "Cam, wake up."

His eyes flutter open and he smiles, a warm gentle expression that softens his face, making me forget where we are, but in two blinks his lips tighten. He sits up. "Have you talked to Katie?"

"No, I just woke up." I push his shoulder. "Go."

He leans over and gives me a quick kiss before running to the stairs.

Dread fills my heart. I should probably go with him but I can't move. I have a horrible feeling that our efforts were pointless. I yank the covers off my legs just as a blood-curdling "Katie!" stops me cold.

I race up the stairs and find Cameron on the bathroom floor cradling Katie in his arms. He looks up at me, tears streaming down his face. "Call 9-1-1!" I run back downstairs and press the numbers, but when the person answers I don't know what to tell her. "We need an ambulance but I don't know the address. Hold on!" I run back upstairs and pound on a closed door. "What's the address here?" I'm breathless, frantic.

The voice on the phone calls out. "Hello? Miss?"

"I'm at a friends house and a girl is unconscious. I'm trying to find out the address."

The door opens and Sarah's mom opens the door. "What's going on?"

"It's Katie. I called 9-1-1 but I don't know your address."

She steps into the hallway, grabs the phone from my hand, and rattles off the address. "Thank you," she says before hanging up. She hands me the phone but keeps her hands on mine. "Tell me what's happened."

"It's Katie." I point at the bathroom and she hurries down the hall. She stops at the doorway. Her hand flutters to her mouth and for a moment she seems frozen, then she disappears into the bathroom. I edge closer to the door but can't bring myself to go inside.

They have Katie on her back. Sarah's mom is breathing into her mouth while Cameron presses her chest, but Katie's face is a ghostly pale color that doesn't look natural. I don't know how much time has passed, but at some point Sarah and Maddy come out of their rooms and stand behind me. We watch, helpless, as Sarah's mom leans against the vanity, her hand resting on Katie's cheek.

"Cam," she whispers. "It's not helping."

"I'm not stopping." He continues pressing the heels of his hands to Katie's chest. Her body jerks with each compression, but her face is lifeless.

Five, ten, I don't know how many minutes later, a thump on the front door makes us all turn. Sarah flies down the stairs and in moments the small space is filled with EMTs. They push us from the room and swirl around Katie, a chaotic dance that ends with them huddled over her body.

The female EMT slides a tube into Katie's throat. Maybe Katie's still alive. The EMT's tiny fingers maneuver the plastic until she's satisfied, then tape it into place. This is so much worse than the first time. It was bad enough knowing what happened, but seeing Katie, seeing what they're doing to her body to try to save her... these images will be burned into my memory forever.

Cameron leans against the doorway, his eyes never leaving his sister. I rest my head on his arm and he slides an arm around me, lowering his head to whisper in my ear. "You have to try again."

I can't say I'm surprised, but my gut still clenches.

"I'll drive you."

"Cam, I don't know. Last time I double flickered they had to crack my skull open."

The EMTs lift Katie onto a stretcher and stand in unison.

He squeezes me tighter and that same spark of fear from last time puts me on my guard. "Look at her. You have to."

Katie is carried down the stairs and we follow silently. The brisk morning air is like a slap in the face. I wrap my arms around myself to keep warm. The driveway is crowded—Sarah's family, me and Cameron, plus a few curious neighbors—but it's obscenely quiet. No one wants to talk about the young girl flirting with death or the reason she's in the ambulance.

When the back doors slam shut and the lights flick on, Cameron turns to me, gripping my shoulders tightly. Red lights flash over his face, coloring his emotions and making him look more menacing than I've ever seen him. "Please, Biz, I'm begging you." He closes his eyes for a moment and he takes a deep breath. "I know I'm asking a lot of you." He presses a kiss to my still-short hair. My shoulder throbs where he released it.

"You know the risks. Look at my dad. And besides, what more can we do?"

He hangs his head and squeezes the bridge of his nose with his fingers. "I know, but I can't lose her. Not again. Not like this."

I don't want to do it. I love Katie, but what about me? My parents?

"I need to go home first."

"Can I pick you up in half an hour?"

"That's not much time."

"Biz, please."

"Fine." I go inside to get my things. When I get back outside, the ambulance, Katie, is gone. My hands shake as I unlock my car. This isn't a good idea, but I feel trapped. I have to do whatever I can to help Katie, but what if it still doesn't work? Some things have a way of happening no matter what I do, and if she's determined to take her life, I won't be able to stop her.

At home I knock lightly on my parents' bedroom door, then lean inside. "Dad," I whisper. "Can you come here a minute?"

He follows me downstairs and I explain what's going on.

His light eyes are watery and he seems to have lost even more weight since yesterday. "Are you sure you want to do this?"

I shake my head, setting loose a fresh wave of tears.

"Then don't."

I wipe my eyes with my sleeve. "I don't feel like I have a choice."

He touches my head, much like Cameron did, but here I feel safe, protected. "You always have a choice. I know you love Cam and his family, but what happens afterward? You have your future to think about. And me and Mom."

I lean into his embrace. "I am."

"But you're going to do it."

I nod.

He presses a kiss to my forehead. "I love you.

"I love you, too."

I run upstairs to change clothes, then wait outside for Cameron, dreading whatever will happen next.

Chapter 38

Cameron grips the steering wheel so hard his knuckles are white and I'm pretty sure he hasn't blinked since he picked me up.

"Are you sure you're okay to drive?"

He glances at me. "We need to save Katie."

"I know, but if we crash before I flicker..."

He loosens his grip and rolls his head from side to side. "I'm fine."

We're only a few miles from the Strand. With each passing second the feeling that I shouldn't be doing this grows stronger. What if I end up in the hospital again? Or worse? I want to go to college and become a famous photographer and get married and maybe have babies someday. By the time we round the bend and the trees come into view, the voice in my head is screaming to stop the car and get out, get out, get out.

"Cam, I don't want to do this."

He jerks his head at me then looks back at the road. "What are you talking about? You're her only chance!"

"I know, but what about me? What if this hurts me worse than last time?" I pick at the seam of my jeans. The words barely come out. "I don't want to die."

If he hears me, he doesn't show it.

Tears burn my eyes and I slide my hand toward the door handle. I run my thumb over the cool metal, scenes from the past few weeks flashing through my mind: Nate pushing me and calling me names, Christina making me feel stupid about my hair, Sarah and whatever she has going on with Cameron. But despite all that, I like my life. I'm not ready to give it up. "You realize I might not be able to stop her, right? That we could both die?"

Cameron takes a breath. "You'll be fine. I trust you."

I bite my lip. He's not even making sense at this point. "I think you're in shock."

The car speeds up. He's not listening. I'm risking my

health—possibly my life—for him, but he doesn't care what happens to me.

I close my eyes when the light starts flashing through the windows, but my fingers and toes start tingling anyway. "I'm scared," I whisper, and Cameron grabs my hand. I try to shake him off but he's holding too tightly. The heaviness comes quickly, then the lightness, then—

—I'm at my locker between classes. Cameron is leaning on the locker next to mine.

"Will this day ever end?" I look in my locker, not sure which book to grab. "What class is next?"

Cameron straightens, staring at the kids in the hallway. His mouth falls open and, oddly, the vacant expression from the car is still on his face. "What the hell is going on?"

"What do you mean?" I know I don't need to pretend since Cameron knows that I flicker, but it's habit to act like nothing happened.

"Is this what it's always like?" His head seems to be on a swivel, swinging back and forth at everything around us.

I touch his arm. "I'm not following."

He moves closer. "Biz, I flickered with you."

I stumble back. "What? How? That's impossible."

He gestures at himself, waving his hands over his body. "You tell me."

"I wonder..." He must have still been touching me. Before Amelia drove me yesterday—today—I'd never considered if that was even possible, but it must be.

Cameron's eyes are wide, waiting.

"All I can think is it's because we were touching when I flickered." I try to recall every time I flickered over the past four years, but there are too many to count. I was usually by myself, or else trying to conceal it from whoever I was with. Except for when Cameron drove me to stop Turner, no one ever knew what was happening.

He studies his hands, turning them over like they aren't a part of him, then raises his eyes. There's a light in them that wasn't there a moment ago. "Let's go find Katie." He's moving down the hall before I have a chance to answer. I slam my locker shut and hurry after him.

He drives the short distance to the middle school, parking in the visitor lot out front.

"How are you going to get her out of class? They won't let you just walk in there."

He yanks open the heavy steel door. "I'm on the approved list of people that can pick her up. I had to take her to doctor's appointments a couple times so they know who I am."

Another thing I somehow don't know.

He steps into the office and it's like he flips a switch, revealing the charming, slightly brooding boy I fell in love with. He leans on the counter separating the ladies working in the office from the public and smiles.

They beam at him and I hold back a laugh.

"What can we do for you?" the younger one asks.

He clears his throat. Only I know that's a sign of nervousness. "I need to get my sister out of class. We have a family emergency at home."

The older lady jumps into action. "James, right?"

"Yeah." He hands her his ID and she scans it with a handheld gizmo before eyeing me.

"Oh, right." I dig my ID out of my bag and hand it to her.

She smiles as she clicks the keyboard at the corner of the desk. "Katie's in Mr. Connor's class. American History. Room 17." She scribbles a note on the pad near the computer, then hands it to Cameron. "I hope everything's okay."

He takes the note and holds it like it's the key to keeping Katie alive. "Thanks. I do, too."

I give an awkward wave to the ladies then follow him down the hall. "That was way easier than I expected."

He shrugs, never slowing his pace. "They like me in there."

I snort. "You could say that."

We stop at a second steel door and wait until the secretary buzzes us through, then Cameron pulls the door open. I feel like we're stepping into a high-security prison, not a middle school full of pimply, pre-pubescent kids.

We round a corner and Cameron comes to a sudden stop. He knocks on the window of the door marked 17. Mr. Connor looks at us without stopping writing on the board. He nods once, but continues talking. After what feels like hours he finally comes to the door.

"What do you need?"

Cameron thrusts the note at him. "My sister, Katie."

Mr. Connor scans the note then turns to the class. "Miss James, please grab your things and come here."

Katie appears at the door, bag over her shoulder, a mildly curious expression on her face. "Busting me out?"

I resist the urge to pull her into my arms.

"Mom and Dad need us at home." He glances at the note and Katie follows his gaze. "Let's go."

Mr. Connor closes the door behind us and we head to the parking lot.

"What's this really about?"

"We'll tell you when we get home."

"Oh yay." The sarcasm drips from her voice and I'm struck again by how much older she seems. Once we're in the car she drops the attitude. "So what's this really about?"

Cameron's eyes don't leave the road. Perhaps it's easier for him to be honest with Katie if he's not looking at her. "We're worried about you."

She rolls her eyes. "What else is new?"

He stretches his fingers over the steering wheel, glancing in the rearview mirror to look at her. "We know what you're planning to do."

"How do you—" she stops with a huff. "Whatever. You don't know anything."

"I know you're planning to take Maddy's mom's sleeping pills."

She shifts, digging her leg into the back of my seat. "Why

would I do that?"

"Katie, we're not going to let you hurt yourself."

She's quiet for a long time. As we're turning onto their street she whispers under her breath, "You can't stop me."

Chapter 39

If I thought waiting at Sarah's was torture, then this is a heartbreaking agony like I've never experienced. Katie refuses to speak to us. I pulled up the suicide prevention website on my phone and Cameron tried every variation they suggest, but nothing is getting through to her. Right now we're staring at the TV while Katie sits, arms crossed, in the chair across the room.

"Can I try?" I whisper in his ear.

He shrugs.

I lean forward. "Katie, your family is worried about you. I'm worried about you."

She turns her head so I can see her roll her eyes. "Good cop, bad cop?"

"That depends on which one you think I am."

She smirks, and that small reaction feels like a huge victory. Then she speaks. "I don't know why you think your opinion even matters. Just because you're dating my brother doesn't mean you're my friend."

"That's not true. I've loved you like a sister for practically your whole life. Have you forgotten all the time we used to spend together, or have you just blocked it out? Because you're more to me than just someone's little sister." My heart races. Even though I said these exact words before, they don't feel any less true. If we can save her, whatever happens to me might be worth it.

The harshness around her eyes softens, but just for a moment. "Anything you have to say to me is pointless."

I pause. This didn't work before but I did get through to her for a minute. "What if I tell you that I'm the reason you were rescued?"

"Rescued? You mean brought from one hell to another? Sure, I'm not being raped anymore but the shit inside my head doesn't go away just because I'm back in my old room. I'll never be able to undo what he did, and nothing you or my family says or does is going to change that."

Cameron inhales sharply next to me.

Katie's words are identical, but the ferociousness isn't the same as it was in Maddy's room. It's as if she somehow can sense that she's lived this before and no longer has the energy to fight.

But I need her to fight.

Katie glares at me. "This is why I don't like being here. I feel like I'm constantly being watched, like people are wondering what exactly he did to me and if I'm finally going to snap. Even you. Right now I can see the wheels turning, waiting, watching. Always wondering when I'm going to go off the deep end."

I wait for a beat to take a breath. Hearing this for a second time doesn't take away the surprise at how much pain she feels. "You don't have to like me, but I care about you. You've been like my sister my entire life and I'm asking you not to do anything stupid. If you do," I pause to take another breath, "he wins."

She seems to consider this, and for a moment I think I might have broken through, but her face crumples. Again. "Don't you get it? He's already won." Tears threaten to spill but she no longer seems to care.

"No, Katie, that's not true." I start to move toward her, then sit back down. This is where I screwed up last time.

"But he has. Look at me. I'm broken." She looks down at herself and seems to recoil at what she sees. "Whatever was good in me is gone."

I need her to get angry. "I don't believe that. That's him talking. And you can't let him win."

She wipes her eyes with her sleeve, then folds her arms tightly across her chest, cocooning herself from the world. Her head shakes slowly from side to side.

I bite my tongue. I'm out of ideas but I know we need to keep her talking.

Cameron sniffs next to me, then wipes his own eyes. "Katie, I just got you back. If you won't do it for yourself, will you do it for me?"

She stares at him for several moments, considering his words. Then slowly, like clouds moving out after a storm, the hard expression on her face softens and she approaches Cameron, who rises to give her a hug. "I'm sorry," she says. He cradles her head against his chest and they rock together until she pulls away and moves toward the stairs.

He faces me. "I don't know how I can thank you."

How do I tell him that I don't think we're out of the

proverbial woods just yet?

"I know I forced you to do this, but it was worth it, right?" The past couple hours have left him an emotional wreck and the stoic expression that normally shields his feelings has dropped away, leaving a little boy desperate for forgiveness.

I reach for his hand. "I hope so." I'm not convinced that Katie isn't still going to try to kill herself, and if she does, I will have risked my life for nothing. I don't know if I can forgive Cameron for that. If I'm even here to forgive him. "We should call Martinez just in case. If you recall, the last time I flickered inside a flicker I ended up having brain surgery."

His mouth falls open. "But you were back to the present, weren't you?"

I shake my head gently, already anticipating the headache that might make my head actually explode.

His knees buckle and he sinks onto the couch. "I didn't know."

I sit next to him, resting my hand on his cheek. "You were desperate to get Katie back. I know that."

His eyes well with tears. "Biz, I'm so sorry. I never meant to hurt you."

"I know." I swallow his apology, hoping it's enough.

We're still on the couch when his parents come home. Neither of us pay attention to the movie playing on the TV, but we're not talking either, each lost in our thoughts. Several times I've started to suggest we drag Katie back down here and force her to watch TV with us, if for no other reason than if she's sitting arms' reach away, maybe we can keep her safe.

Mr. James breaks the silence. "Has Katie been upstairs all afternoon?"

"Yeah," Cameron says.

I nudge him to say more. His parents need to know what's going on.

He runs his hand over his mouth. "She's been—she's having a hard time lately."

Mrs. James leans forward. "More than usual?"

"Yeah. We're worried about her."

Mrs. James studies us for a beat before facing her husband. "We shouldn't have let her stop seeing the therapist." She bites her lip. "I think we should go talk to her."

"Now?"

"Yes, now. I'm glad you kids told us that you're worried. It's too easy to just hope things will get better on their own."

They move as one to check on Katie. I hear several knocks, but the door never opens.

"Katie," Mr. James says. Then more urgently. "Katie?"

My stomach drops. What if they're too late? All this time I've assumed that Katie took the sleeping pills from Sarah's mom, but what if she already has them? I race up the stairs, Cameron close on my heels.

"What is it?"

"Did you check her bag for the pills?"

He stops suddenly and his face goes white. "No."

Together we approach her room, standing behind his parents. His dad opens the door a crack, then rushes inside, his mom right behind him. An animal wail, then a scream, pierces the silence.

I fall to the floor.

It didn't work.

Cameron moves past me into her room as his dad calls 9-1-1. He's a lot more collected than I was when I called, but his voice breaks at the end. "Please h-hurry. She's not breathing."

A dissonant chorus of sobs and whimpers sound in the room, punctuated by Mrs. James's high-pitched voice murmuring "Katie." I peek into the room. Her parents are huddled around

Katie's body on the floor while Cameron alternates between chest compressions and breathing into her mouth. I want to tell him it's pointless, that no matter what he does, she's going to die. It's what she wants.

I back away from the door and go downstairs to wait for the ambulance. It doesn't take long. I open the door to a different set of EMTs and point them up the stairs, then pace the small hallway. A niggling voice tells me to call Martinez, and I glance at the stairs. Katie's death was devastating the first time, and nearly swallowed me whole the second. This time I feel numb. I've done everything I can. Now I need to do whatever I can to make sure I don't join her.

Chapter 40

I remember Katie as a child, leaping down the stairs, pretending she could fly, her dreams changing on a daily basis. Now those dreams are over, and she's being carried down those same stairs on a stretcher, straps across her chest and legs and an oxygen mask over her nose. Her parents follow close behind, with Cameron a few steps after them. The procession moves past me to the driveway, where the open doors of the ambulance beckon. The medics gently lift the stretcher inside, treating her as delicately as a newborn.

The pressure in my chest is unbearable. I approach Cameron and wrap an arm around his waist. "Cam, I'm so sorry."

He looks at me, face streaked with tears. While he doesn't

remember the first time, his grief now is great enough to make up for it. "You have to do something."

I shake my head. There's nothing left to do.

"You have to go back and save Katie!"

My mouth falls open. I can't believe he's asking me again. I loosen my grip on his side and take a step back. "I can't."

His jaw clenches. "You mean you won't."

"Do you know what you're asking?" I'm worried about getting to the hospital in time and he wants me to go back again? "Cam, I can't."

"If you loved me—"

I shove my hands against his chest. "You know this might kill me! It's already killed my dad and you don't even care!" I pace in a tight circle. I can't look at him. "I'm the flicker expert, not you."

"I care." He sounds defeated, but it doesn't lessen my anger.

I whirl on him. "Most of the time the things I change end up happening anyway. I could go back a thousand times and Katie will still end up in that ambulance." I flail my arm at the ambulance just as the siren squeals, and we both jump.

The lights turn on, casting a red glow over his face, bouncing off the side of the house. He watches as it pulls out of the driveway.

His parents are already in their car. His dad rolls down the window. "Cam, are you coming?"

Cameron meets my eyes and I shake my head again. He closes his eyes for a moment and when he opens them, his expression is cold, hard. He calls over his shoulder. "I'm coming."

I look around the driveway, frantic. He's leaving me here? How am I supposed to get to the hospital? Cameron is climbing into the backseat when I shout, "Wait!"

He pauses, a glimmer of hope on his face.

"Can I come, too?"

The hope fades as he slides into the car.

I hurry to the other side and climb in.

We follow the ambulance through the neighborhood, and I'm reminded of the last time mom and I followed an ambulance to the hospital. That's the night Dad nearly broke my jaw during a seizure. It's also the night I met Martinez.

Martinez!

I pull out my phone and text him a cryptic message. I don't know if the hospital monitors his phone but it can't hurt to be cautious. His reply comes quickly.

> Martinez: Ride along tonight. Be at the hos-
> pital in half hour.

Next I text Dad.

> Me: Heading to hospital. Double flickered.
> Martinez is on his way.

I lean my head against the back of the seat and close my eyes.

By the time we arrive at the hospital, Cameron's mom is crying so hard that I'm worried she won't be able to get out of the car. Mr. James parks behind the ambulance in the covered area near the emergency entrance, then opens the door and yells while running toward the doors. "Can someone help my wife?" He catches a woman in scrubs on their way to the ambulance but she shakes him off and continues to Katie's ambulance.

Cameron and I get out of the car, leaving his mom sobbing in the front seat. The lights from the ambulance bounce off the white concrete so I lower my chin and shield my eyes as I run inside. I don't have time for a fake-flicker. Cameron stands by the ambulance, hands on his head, while his dad goes back to the car to help his mom.

I rush to the receiving desk. "Can someone help my boyfriend's mom? Her daughter's the one in the ambulance and I think she's having a breakdown or something."

The woman behind the desk speaks into the phone, then nods. "They'll be right out."

I walk back to the doors as they're pulling Katie from the ambulance. Mr. James is kneeling by his wife but looks frantically at Katie. He stands as they push her toward the doors, Cameron at her side. When they wheel her inside I slip through the doors and go over to the car. "Go with Katie. I'll wait with her."

"Are you sure?"

"Yes, go."

He touches his wife's face, then sprints after the gurney.

If I stare into the car the flashing lights aren't so bad. Mrs. James's sobs have quieted but tears stream down her face and the light in her eyes is gone. How much grief can a person handle before they completely go off the deep end? I reach for her hand and squeeze her fingers, but she doesn't react. I move a lock of hair off her cheek and her focus shifts to me briefly, then she's back to staring at nothing.

I still haven't heard from Dad, which can't be good. I slip my phone from my pocket with my free hand and peck out a message to Mom.

Me: Everything ok?

My phone buzzes as an EMT comes over to the car. My stomach flutters for a second, but it's not Martinez. And why the hell am I having that reaction? I shake it off and back away so he can help her, then check my phone.

Mom: We're at the hospital.

No, not now. Please let Dad be okay. I look up toward the windows, which I could see if I wasn't in the ambulance bay, and the lights finally manage their full assault. My knees crumple and I crash to the pavement. The tingling in my hands is so bad that I drop my phone.

"Miss, are you okay?"

I hang my head to block the light. "Yeah, I'm fine."

He looks uncertain, glancing between me and Mrs. James.

"Help her. I'll get myself inside."

He gently reaches over her to unfasten her seatbelt, then guides her out of the car.

I fumble out a message to mom.

Me: Me too. I'll come find you.

I drag myself to my feet. Everyone I love is inside those doors. Katie is in the ER with her family and an army of doctors, but deep in my gut I know that no matter what they do, it's not enough. I tried, and I failed. Now she's gone.

I straighten.

I've done all I could. It's time to worry about my own family.

Chapter 41

The woman behind the counter in the ER gives me the same sad smile as before. "Can I help you?"

"I just found out my dad is here and I'm hoping you can tell me what room he's in."

She purses her lips. "My, this hasn't been a good day for you, has it?"

"No." I rest my elbows on the counter and lean forward to see her computer screen. "The last name is Clement."

"I'm not supposed to give out that information."

I slap my hand on the counter, making her jump. "Look! This has been a really, really long day and I could use a little help right now."

She stares at me, apparently weighing her options.

"He's. My. Dad. You're not breaking any rules. I'm immediate family." An ER nurse that I've talked to before hurries by and I wave at her. "Excuse me." She stops and looks at us, her stern face softening when she sees me. "Can you please tell—" I look at the woman's name tag "—Ms. Bunting that I'm not going to leak anyone's personal information and that I just need to find my dad?"

She steps closer to the counter. "Janie, get over your power trip and tell her where her dad is." She meets my eyes. "Mr. Clement, right?"

"Yeah."

She glares at Janie.

Janie lets out an exaggerated sigh. "Fine. But if I get in trouble I'm telling them you coerced me." She taps a few keys on the keyboard then squints at the monitor. "Room 231."

Same floor as always. "Thanks," I say to Janie, before turning to the nurse. "And thank you."

She touches my shoulder. "Go find your dad. I hope he's okay."

I turn to leave, then stop. "If you see Martinez, will you tell him where I'm at?"

Her head tilts to one side, then she nods, slowly. "Sure thing."

I hurry to the elevators. There aren't as many people beyond the ER and I ride by myself to the second floor. The halls are dimly lit but I don't need lights to know where I'm going. I pause in the doorway before entering.

Mom sits in a chair pulled tightly against the bed, clutching Dad's hand. Both of them have their eyes closed and I take a moment to collect myself. But stopping allows the past thirty-six hours to catch up to me and a tsunami of emotions nearly sweeps me off my feet. Katie is gone. Maybe not yet, but soon. I tried as hard as I could to save her but it wasn't enough, and I'm afraid she took a piece of me with her this time. And Dad... He looks comfortable, at peace, but I'm not ready for whatever comes next.

A sob breaks free from my chest and Mom opens her eyes.

"Biz." She lifts an arm, calling me to her, and in seconds I'm at her side, my face buried in her lap. She strokes my hair, her fingers working their way to the back of my neck where she starts kneading.

My headache hasn't started yet but I let her continue. Sometimes it's nice just to have someone love you.

"When did you bring him in?"

"Shortly after you left."

I lift my head. "Did he have another seizure?"

She shakes her head.

"Then why didn't either of you tell me he wasn't feeling well?" I know the answer as soon as I ask the question. Because Dad knew I wouldn't try to save Katie.

"You know how proud your father is. He never wants to admit he's sick."

That's because he's not sick. He had a wonderful gift and now it's killing him. Like it might kill me someday. "So what did the doctors say?"

Her lips press together and her eyes well with tears. She rests her hand on my cheek. "The deterioration... it's progressing faster than they thought. The doctor says he doesn't have much longer."

I pull away so I can see him. If you ignore the tubes running up his nose and the IV in his arm, he looks serene, rested. A tear slips past my lashes and I bite my lip to hold back the flood of emotion that threatens to crush me. I reach for his arm and am surprised by how cool he is, but there isn't much left to keep him warm.

His eyes blink open at my touch.

I stand, leaning over Mom so he can see me. A fresh wave of tears threaten and he shakes his head.

"No tears."

"I hate seeing you like this."

He smiles at Mom. "I told her not to bring me here but she insisted."

Her smile wobbles. "I'm not ready to let you go."

"I wish you'd told me before I left for Cam's. I would have stayed with you."

Dad's smile tightens. "You had things to take care of." His eyes narrow. "How did it go?"

I shake my head and his shoulders slump even more than they already are.

"I'm sorry."

Mom sniffles. "What did I miss?"

"I'll fill you in later." I've relived Katie's death too many times. I can't do it again.

Dad takes a moment to absorb my news, then seems to shake it off and his eyes brighten. "I forgot to give you something when you were home." It's not like Dad to forget anything, ever.

I'm struggling to accept that he's really dying, but the changes in him are nearly impossible to deny.

"What is it?"

He looks at Mom, who smiles back at him. "You have mail from several newspapers. My guess is they bought your photos."

"What?" A surge of excitement pushes away thoughts of death and for a second I'm happy.

"We didn't open them," Mom says. "But we wanted you to know." They clasp hands and share a knowing look.

"What?"

Dad smiles. "The fact that you're already having success as a photographer tells us that you definitely need to go to college to pursue this as a career."

My excitement fades as quickly as it came. "But how can I leave you?" I look at Dad, not wanting to say the words, but if I go away to school Mom will be all alone.

She laces her fingers through mine and pulls my hand against her lips. "It will be harder without you at home, but I'll manage."

Dad clears his throat. "I won't let you give up your dreams just because I'm not around to see you make them come true."

Another throat clears at the door and we turn our heads. Martinez is standing in the doorway. He's wearing his EMT uniform—the one he had on the first time we met—and my body does a weird tingling thing that's different from when I flicker.

Dad nods. "Dr. Martinez."

He enters the room and nods at each of my parents, "Mr. Clement, Mrs. Clement," before looking at me. "You needed to see me?"

"Yeah."

Mom starts to get up but I place a hand on her shoulder to stop her. She sinks into her chair with little resistance. "Stay with Dad. We won't be long, then I'll come back." I lean close to Dad to kiss his cheek. "See you soon."

He grabs my hand and squeezes tightly. "I love you."

Tears spring to my eyes, again. "I love you, too." Then I move around the bed and follow Martinez to the elevator.

"What's this about?"

I wait until we're safely inside the elevator before answering, but once there I'm very aware of how close he's standing and how less authoritative he looks when he's not in his white lab coat. I'd forgotten how muscular his arms are and how—

"Biz?"

"Sorry." I blush, hoping he doesn't notice in the poorly lit elevator. "I flickered yesterday, well, tomorrow, then had to flicker again. The timing was pretty close and I'm not sure if I double-flickered or flickered inside a flicker."

He rubs a hand over his face. "You're losing me."

"A double flicker means a killer headache. Flickering inside a flicker means... well... an actual killer headache. That's what landed me in your operating room last time."

His face pales, and the fact that I can see the shift in color makes me blush again, since he must have noticed me blush when I was checking him out. "But you seem fine right now."

"I won't catch up to my present until morning."

"Which is why you need me now."

I sigh, relieved that he's got it. "Yes."

The elevator opens and I follow him to his office. He turns on the light and I hop onto the table like usual, but nothing about this feels normal. Darkness fills the windows where there's normally sunlight, and the small counter is covered in paperwork instead of my file.

And, of course, Martinez does not look like my doctor.

"Let's run through the list." First he checks my pupils and reflexes, then I climb down and do the finger-to-the-nose and other balancing drills. Once I'm back on the table he crosses his arms. "I don't see anything out of the ordinary, but you still seem off. Is everything okay?"

I don't want to get into it with him but I can only stare into his concerned eyes for a few seconds before I burst into tears. He moves closer and gently touches my arm, which makes me cry harder. Why do I lose my shit when people are nice to me? You'd think it'd be the other way around.

"Biz, why did you flicker? What were you trying to fix?"

"Cameron's sister killed herself."

"Oh." It comes out as a puff of air. His eyes narrow.

"I went back to stop her, but she did it again. Then Cameron made me flicker again but she still killed herself. That's why we're here. The last time she did it at their house and her parents found her. I was there when it happened so I rode here with them and that's when I found out my dad was here, too."

He touches the side of my face and peers into my eyes. "I'm surprised you're still standing. Do you want a sedative so you can rest?"

Nothing sounds better, but I can't. Not now. "I need to find Cam. To make sure he's okay."

Martinez leans against the counter and crosses his arms. "Is he aware what could happen to you if you flickered again?"

I nod.

His nostrils flare. "You're worried about him, even though, as you said, he made you flicker knowing full well what it could mean for you?"

I hang my head. I've been trying not to think about that, about what it means for us. "He was worried about his sister."

"Well, I'm worried about you."

I look up and try to read his expression, but he's a stone wall. Jaw clenched, lips tight, brows furrowed. "I've got some time. Let me find him, then I'll come back and you can run your tests and whatnot." I pull out my phone and hold it up. I'd almost forgotten about the video. Even though it's from the first time I flickered, the video is still there since I've had my phone the whole time. "I have something for you."

He raises an eyebrow. If this situation weren't so screwed up—and he wasn't, you know, an adult—I'd swear he's flirting with me. I'm probably imagining any interest on his part.

"I recorded myself flickering."

Now both eyebrows are up. "When?"

"After Katie killed herself. The first time." I extend my hand, offering the phone.

He takes it, and our fingers brush for just a moment. "It could have waited."

"I know, but Amelia was already driving me so I figured I may as well kill two birds with—" I slap a hand over my mouth. "God, that's awful."

He rests a hand on my shoulder. "I know what you mean. Have you watched it?"

"No."

"Can I copy it?"

I should have anticipated this, but his question surprises me. Of course he wants to copy it. What, is he going to borrow my phone whenever he wants to study the video?

I shrug. "Sure."

He turns to the counter behind him and removes a tablet from a drawer. In moments he's connected the devices.

A shudder passes through me. My secret is officially exposed.

He hands me the phone.

I jut my chin at his uniform, trying to shake off the feeling that I've made a terrible mistake. "Are you done for the night or are you supposed to go on more calls?"

"I might do one more before we meet back here. Are you sure you don't need to stay with your dad?"

"I'll stop by his room after I talk to Cam."

"Text me if I'm not back yet."

"Okay." I slide off the table as he steps toward the door, and once again we're standing closer than I intended. He moves around me without making eye contact and in moments we're back in the elevator. When the doors open we step onto the tiled floor, but he grabs my arm, stopping me.

"I know you care about Cameron, but I don't like that he was willing to risk your life to save his sister. He doesn't get to choose whose life is more valuable."

His warm hand sends shivers through me. "I know."

"I'm not sure you do. I admire that you want to help people, but at some point you need to put yourself first. The trick is not letting anyone make you feel bad for doing so." He releases my arm and straightens his uniform. "I'll see you soon." He walks away, his strong shoulders pulled back, arms swinging at his sides.

I should go find Cameron, but I find myself glued to this spot. The last thing Cameron said to me was a challenge that if I loved him, I'd risk my life for Katie's. He knows what that could mean for me and no matter how many times I tell myself that it was his grief for Katie talking, I can't ignore the fact that he's willing to take that risk. That he'd be okay with me dying.

I lean against the wall and sink to the floor, my back pressed against the cold marble. While it's true that I don't want to leave Mom alone, I haven't wanted to admit that I'm also afraid to leave Cameron. Aside from Amelia, he knows me better than anyone and the thought of him no longer being a part of my life makes it feel like the air's been sucked from the room, leaving me gasping for breath on the floor.

Long-distance romances never work, no matter how many kids at school seem to think they do, and the more states between me and Cameron the less likely we are to stay together.

But maybe that's a good thing. Earlier, when I asked Cameron how you can put a price on your own life, I didn't expect an answer, but his actions spoke for him. Maybe it's time I start looking out for myself.

If I've learned anything from what's happened, it's that

going back in time can't always save the future. Repeating the same mistakes over and over doesn't change anything.

I push myself to my feet and press the button for the elevator. Once on the second floor I pause to take a deep breath.

For the first time in a long time I've made a decision for me, and it feels right.

Referenced Sources

Feeling hopeless, useless, or unloved—like there's no reason to go on living—is more common than you think. No matter how desperate things may seem, you are not alone. If you or someone you know is struggling with thoughts of suicide, there are sources online to help you.

These are the websites Biz and Amelia visited when they tried to help Katie:

www.suicidepreventionlifeline.org
www.samhsa.gov

Suicide Prevention Dialogue with Consumers and Survivors: From Pain to Promise (Substance Abuse and Mental Health Services Administration)

U.S. DEPARTMENT OF HEALTH AND HUMAN SERVICES, Substance Abuse and Mental Health Services Administration, Center for Mental Health Services

Acknowledgments

Many people helped me journey into the world of a sequel:

Nadine, your enthusiasm and unwavering belief in me and my writing means the world to me. I couldn't imagine writing without you by my side—even if you're on the other side of the country.

Stacey, I can't put into words how much I value our friendship. Your laughter and support keep me going, while your penchant for the things that scare the living bejeezus out of me keeps me on my toes.

Erica, thank you for not being afraid to be honest, even when it may not be what I want to hear. I can only hope everyone has a writing friend like you.

A deep, heartfelt thank you to Nancy, whose tireless efforts made this book the best it could be. Mentioning you here doesn't do justice for the amount of time and effort you put into helping me, including the character exercises where our MCs chatted in a bar. Thank you.

As always, thank you to my mother, Judy, for being my first, last, and most nit-picky reader. My novels wouldn't be the same without you.

Thank you to my husband, Jeremy. Your love, support, and understanding, while sounding cliché, are anything but. I truly couldn't do this without you.

And finally, a big thank you to my readers. Hearing from you and knowing how much you've looked forward to the sequel kept me going through the many, many drafts. I hope it's been worth the wait.

Coming in 2015

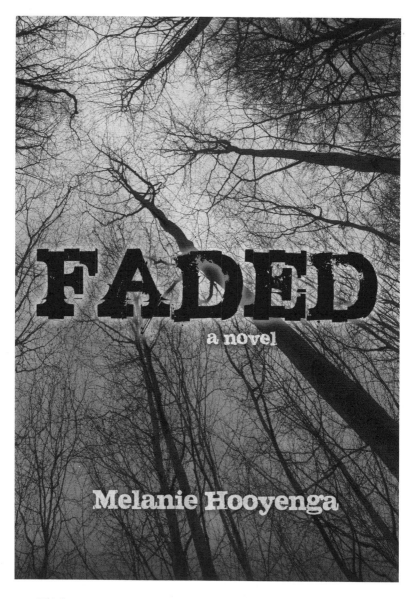

FADED

a novel

Melanie Hooyenga

Flickering can't undo what you've already caused.

About the Author

Melanie Hooyenga first started writing as a teenager and finds she still relates best to that age group. Her young-adult novel, FLICKER, debuted in November 2012.

She has lived in Washington DC, Chicago, and Mexico, but has finally settled down in her home state of Michigan with her husband Jeremy. When not at her day job as a graphic designer, you can find Melanie attempting to wrangle her Miniature Schnauzer Owen and playing every sport imaginable with Jeremy.